All the Bold Days
of My Restless Life

All the Bold Days of
My Restless Life

Sharon Stone

los angeles

Celebrating Twenty-Five Years

MANUFACTURED IN THE UNITED STATES OF AMERICA.

THIS TRADE PAPERBACK ORIGINAL IS PUBLISHED BY ALYSON BOOKS, P.O. BOX 4371, LOS ANGELES, CALIFORNIA 90078-4371.
DISTRIBUTION IN THE UNITED KINGDOM BY TURNAROUND PUBLISHER SERVICES LTD.,
UNIT 3, OLYMPIA TRADING ESTATE, COBURG ROAD, WOOD GREEN, LONDON N22 6TZ ENGLAND.

FIRST EDITION: MAY 2005

05 06 07 08 09 **a** 10 9 8 7 6 5 4 3 2 1

ISBN 1-55583-908-8
ISBN-13 978-1-55583-908-6

LIBRARY OF CONGRESS CATALOGING-IN-PUBLICATION DATA
STONE, SHARON, 1955–
ALL THE BOLD DAYS OF MY RESTLESS LIFE / SHARON STONE.—1ST ED.
ISBN 1-55583-908-8; ISBN-13 978-1-55583-908-6
1. TELEVISION AUTHORSHIP—FICTION. 2. WOMEN DRAMATISTS—FICTION. 3. SOAP OPERAS—FICTION. 4. LESBIANS—FICTION. I. TITLE.
PS3619.T683A79 2005
813'.6—DC22   2005041032

CREDITS
COVER PHOTOGRAPHY BY TIM HALL/PHOTODISC GREEN/GETTY IMAGES.
COVER DESIGN BY MATT SAMS.

Acknowledgments

I'd like to thank the writers, cast, and crew of *One Life to Live* for allowing me into their wacky little world for a day—which was all I needed to set me off on this wild ride.

For Puddin

Chapter One

"Did you ever have one of those days where the tag was on your toe and the drawer was closing shut?"

The limp body of Bailey Connors slumped against the doorway to her office as she held up a pink phone message between two fingers for Peter Dalton to see. "I've been summoned to Fitzsimmons's office," she snarled.

Peter took in an audible gasp, and his eyes sprang from their sockets upon hearing the name. Fitzsimmons was head of the Standards and Practices Division at NBS—the office that reviewed every word uttered on every television program the network aired, checking scripts for verbal obscenities and obscene interaction between characters. As far as Peter knew, no one on the entire staff of this 30-year-old daytime drama had ever *seen* Fitzsimmons. He had been only a name—a single name at the end of a phone line or signed at the bottom of a memo—a name that wreaked havoc on the human body, doing terrible things to one's vital signs, much like the name Dracula or Frankenstein.

"What did you do this time?" Peter asked, genuinely concerned for his boss.

"I don't know," Bailey lamented, glancing at the clock behind her desk, which said 9:50. She tossed her black canvas shoulder bag on the cluttered desk but kept on her coat. "Shit! Of all the days for me to be late!" she cried as she hurried toward the door. "Go on to the meeting without me—I'll be there as soon as I can!" she shouted over her shoulder at her senior writer as she hustled down the hall, then down the second-floor stairs.

Across 84th Street just off Central Park West, Bailey dashed into the six-story converted brownstone that housed several of the network's departments just below the executive level. The executive offices, naturally, were located in a posh high-rise on the Avenue of the Americas.

She was shown into Fitzsimmons's top-floor suite by his secretary and there discovered not only a bespectacled geezer in a well-tailored suit and bow tie sitting behind a huge mahogany desk, but also Mike Mahoney, producer of *All the Bold Days of My Restless Life,* who was standing in front of a wall of windows. The presence of her direct supervisor shocked her enough; the fact that Mike was wearing a suit instead of his regular jeans and sneakers—and had actually dug his briefcase out of the closet—tipped Bailey off that something was definitely up.

Suddenly her stomach felt like a plum in a Ronco food dehydrator, instantly crinkling into a prune. This had all the earmarks of an ambush, and she suspected she was about to be fired. Fuck. And she had just bought that beautiful condo within walking distance of the office. Oh, well...a condo on Central Park West would be easy to resell.

Fitzsimmons scrutinized the stocky woman from head to toe as she removed her coat and hung it on the rack by the door. He didn't approve of women wearing jeans and flannel shirts and boots to work, not even in a New York winter. In his day, ladies wore dresses— period. And such a large-framed woman would certainly look a lot more feminine if she didn't wear her hair so short. And when did makeup go out of style? Good Lord, was this woman trying to be unattractive? Bah! He would never understand the female sex.

"Aren't you usually in at 9:30?" he asked, his upper-class Philadelphia accent emphasizing his scolding tone.

Bailey shrugged as she sat on the couch against the wall near the door. "Well, yes, but...I had some unexpected personal business to deal with this morning," she said, her eyes cast downward.

Having made his point, Fitzsimmons saw no reason to delve further into the subject, especially if she was talking about "women's troubles"—he certainly did not want to hear about *that*—so he got to the point of the meeting.

"I've called you both here today because of a line of dialogue in your show slated for taping on January 4. It is a scene where Rambo Rodriguez, the psycho killer, sees his next intended victim, RuWanda, the black transvestite hooker with a heart of gold, for the first time and discovers his job will be made that much easier because of RuWanda's temporary vision condition caused by a reaction to her new contact lens solution."

He handed a page from the script to Mike, who scanned the paper until he came to the highlighted text:

"Great! The bitch is blind!"

Fitzsimmons handed Mike another sheet of paper. *"This* was my response to Miss Connors."

"After six years as head writer of All the Bold Days of My Restless Life, *you know NBS does not allow that word in daytime programming. Please replace with a more politically correct term."*

"Here is Miss Connors's rewrite," he said dryly, handing Mike a third sheet, also with highlighted text:

"Great! The bitch is visually impaired!"

A spit-laugh escaped from Mike, but he quickly pulled out a handkerchief and coughed into it a couple of times. "A little cold coming on," he said, as though his state of health were nothing to be concerned about.

He stepped behind Fitzsimmons and faced the windows again, smiling to himself. This was classic Bailey—never passing up the opportunity for a clever

4

line. Then he glanced over his shoulder at the woman sitting on the couch, hands folded in a subservient fashion, and felt a little sorry for the kid, having to sit there and suffer this drubbing. He certainly couldn't fault her for getting a wild hair—hell, if he had to deal with the stodgy censors on a daily basis the way she did, he probably couldn't resist lipping off on paper once in a while too. He caught another snicker in his handkerchief.

"I don't appreciate being mocked, young lady," the elder man said, peering over the top of his glasses at the 38-year-old young lady cowering on the couch. "Nor do I appreciate my valuable time being wasted in such a frivolous manner," he said directly to Mike, whom he felt should have better control over his underlings. "Why don't you just use the word 'witch' instead?" he suggested impatiently.

Bailey shot a quick look at Mike. "We can't," she said timidly.

"Why on earth not?" Fitzsimmons demanded.

"Because of The Patricia Letters," she explained.

Fitzsimmons's face drew up into a contorted scowl of confusion. Bailey gave Mike the "helpless hands" gesture, asking him to explain.

"About a year ago, we had started using 'witch' instead of 'bitch' fairly regularly for one particular character, but then we started getting letters from Patricia Kennealy threatening to organize a national boycott of the show, so we backed down," he said.

"Who the hell is Patricia Kennealy?" Fitzsimmons shouted in a cantankerous tone.

"She's the widow—or former lover—of Jim Morrison, depending on your views of marriage," Mike replied.

"And who the devil is Jim Morrison?"

"A rock star. Well, a dead rock star, now. He OD'd on drugs in a Paris hotel bathroom. Patricia is a self-proclaimed witch, and she and Jim were 'married' in a Wiccan ceremony by a high priestess. Some say it was legal...some say it wasn't," he said with a shrug.

Bailey sat up. "Some also say it wasn't a drug over-dose that he died from but a form of cancer, which in this case was cancer of the penis he supposedly got from repeated bouts of gonorrhea from all the groupies he had sex with," she stated.

"True," Mike replied, "but then there are those who say he had gotten back together with his first wife, Pam, and his witch wife killed him by voodoo or some occult death spell for revenge."

Fitzsimmons's face had mutated from confusion to horror as he turned back and forth from Bailey to Mike. "Are we talking about characters on the show or real people?"

Mike stifled a laughed. "Real people, sir."

"Amazing," the old man said as he shook it off.

"Anyway," Mike continued, "Patricia threatened to hold a string of press conferences and stir up a bunch of bad publicity for the show, and with Jim still being a cult hero to a lot of people, we figured she could prob-ably do it and that it wasn't worth the fight."

Fitzsimmons threw up his hands. "Well, it's your problem to work out, Miss Connors," he said. "You have two weeks until taping to do a proper rewrite. See if you can do it without the humor this time," he added sternly.

Bailey got up to leave, fully expecting Fitzsimmons to warn her not to run with scissors either, and grabbed her coat as Mike approached. "Walk you down to the network meeting," he offered, which Bailey took as an appeasement for what she had just had to endure.

While hustling down the stairs, Bailey couldn't resist commenting on Mike's unusual attire. "And don't you look like a big boy today," she gushed like a proud mommy. "You and your little Fisher-Price briefcase," she added, thunking the leather case on its side with her middle finger. Mike turned beet-red, but he knew he was no match for Bailey and her quick wit and didn't even try to redeem his manhood.

Inside Room 560, which was the office of Sam Ryerson, the spineless senior vice president of daytime programming everyone on the show referred to as "Slinky" Ryerson, the regular Monday 10 o'clock meeting was under way with six of the network executives from advertising, legal, and daytime programming; this was their time to give reviews and suggestions on completed scripts. Mike and Bailey took a seat next to Peter, a 32-year-old refugee screenwriter from Hollywood who, as senior breakdown writer and Bailey's right-hand man, also attended the meetings.

After almost three hours of statistics and suggestions being hurled at Bailey, her head was swimming as usual from doing her standard "mechanical dog in the rear window of a car," bobbing incessantly in agreement with their frequent, inane ideas. When the last item on the agenda had been settled, everyone congratulated themselves on a most productive meeting that, for a change, had ended on time, precisely at 1 o'clock.

"Well, that's it for today, then," Mike said, sounding quite pleased.

"Uh, actually," Sam said sheepishly, having stealthily taken refuge behind his desk, "there is one more thing I need to talk to you about...Bailey."

The dark-haired woman, halfway to her feet, froze in a squat over her chair. Something in Sam's voice indicated this was going to be more bad news.

Suddenly it was a Marx Brothers scramble of arms and legs as Mike and the other executives all tried to be the first out the door to make sure they didn't get hit by any shrapnel from the bomb about to drop. A confused Peter, with his skinny arms and legs, didn't stand a chance and got swept out along with the brothers.

It was obvious to the one left behind that all the executives already knew what was coming. Bailey sat back down, but when Sam hesitated a good 10 seconds after the room had cleared, an alarm went off inside her. She braced herself for a doozy.

Sam sat down and tapped his fingers on his desk a few seconds longer, then grabbed hold of the edges with both hands, took in a deep breath, and looked Bailey square in the eye. "You've got to kill off Binaca."

First, Bailey's jaw hit the floor, then she went into her John McEnroe impersonation. "You can*not* be serious!" she shouted, storming Sam's desk. He pushed back his chair until it hit the wall. "Binaca Blaylock is one of the best villains in the history of daytime drama! Our ratings have *doubled* in the six months she's been on the show! Whose bonehead idea was *this?!*" she demanded, coming completely out of her shell now that someone was messing with her show—her baby.

"Derek forced the issue," Sam quickly confessed, hoping she'd back off.

Bailey shook her head at the pathetic creature from whom these words had wormed their way. She wanted to call him a big pussy for not putting up a fight but felt sure her choice of words would be vetoed by Orville Redenbacher upstairs.

Derek. It figured.

Derek Young had played Chauncey "Ace" Atkinson, second-generation owner and publisher of *The Sun* newspaper in the soap's mythical town of Fairview, since the first episode. He had been a knockout hunk of 29 when he started on the show and had matured into a silver-haired but still virile town patriarch and ladies man. And like his character, Derek had preferred the role of playboy and never married. Some said it was because he subconsciously envisioned himself as the suave Ace Atkinson, which wasn't too far from the truth.

He was the son of a wealthy Manhattan philanthropist and a banker's daughter, both of whom had been part of the upper echelon of New York society, having been on the board of the ballet, the opera, a hospital or two, and a library before they retired and moved to East Hampton. Derek was also considered a god by daytime drama fans, whose ardor for the man surprisingly had grown over the decades...at about the same pace as his ego. But he and Morgan Gable, who played Binaca, clashed from day 1.

Morgan had at one time been the grande dame of Hollywood and today was one of the few remaining icons from the end of the golden era of movies, when she had been a child star. A two-time Oscar winner and a six-time divorcee, she had long borne the reputation of being temperamental and difficult, and at this point in her life, she didn't even bother trying to hide her rough edges. She had paid her dues in this business—now it was her turn to enjoy the fruits of her suffering and give that suffering back as best she could.

And when she wanted something done her way, it was done her way. Many times she had gone up to Bailey's office and addressed the head writer face to face to discuss a change she wanted in a show's dialogue—something none of the other actors had ever lowered themselves to do, preferring to use Mike as a liaison. And more often than not, Bailey had found the actor's instincts to be right.

Morgan Gable wasn't the easiest actor Bailey had ever worked with, but then, neither was Derek. He was just like Morgan—cock of the walk in his domain, always wanting things done his way. Unfortunately, his way was never the same as her way, so it was only natural that the King of Daytime Drama and the Queen of the Silver Screen had clashed when she joined the show as owner of *The Tribune,* a new rival newspaper. Derek's ego had bruised like an overripe banana at having the spotlight taken away—and by a woman, no less.

On the other hand, Morgan had at first bristled over the sexist, impotent female role she had originally been thrust into as the rival newspaper owner who was supposed to get scooped constantly by Ace's community-favorite newspaper. But she had managed to persuade Bailey to gradually transform Binaca into an independent, strong, and at times devious female adversary who scooped Ace on a regular basis, which the viewers loved...and Derek, of course, hated.

The fan mail also had taken a significant shift after Binaca Blaylock came to Fairview and blossomed, and Derek had made no bones about his disdain for this new leading lady who was fiercely crowding his spotlight. Fortunately for Bailey, she was able to deal with these clashes from the periphery, trying to give each actor the same amount of camera time and lines. But poor Mike—he was caught right in the middle most times, down on the set. He had credited his first gray hairs to the two actors and their daily arguments on the set, which occasionally resulted in a prop having to be swept into a trash bin and replaced. All of which made Derek's actions less of a surprise.

Bailey glared at Sam. "What happened?" she asked.

"Derek went to Stubblefield and gave him an ultimatum," Sam explained. "It was either dump a veteran character who's won five Daytime Emmys and has had immense popularity for 30 years or boot the newcomer, whose character was only intended to be a short-term addition to the show anyway."

Bailey still couldn't believe it. She knew both actors were a major pain in the butt, but Morgan was hands down the most talented actor the show had ever seen, and Bailey had learned a lot about dialogue and character development during Morgan's short tenure. The writer was genuinely sorry to say goodbye to both Morgan and Binaca. "So how long does she have to live, Doc?" she said sarcastically.

"Five months. We want you to kill her off for the May sweeps, which is right before the Daytime Emmys. It'll be good publicity and may help garner us an extra statuette or two."

Bailey flashed a big smirk. "Always thinking about the good of the show."

This raised Sam's hackles. "I had no choice," he said as firmly as he could, yet his voice still quavered. "When the head of daytime programming barks, I jump—it's that simple."

Sam pulled out a pink bottle of Pepto-Bismol and swigged directly from the bottle. He replaced the cap and sighed contentedly, like an alcoholic who had just had his first shot of whiskey for the day.

Bailey rolled her eyes, but then she realized Sam truly didn't have a choice under these circumstances and let out a sigh too, along with the rest of her anger. "Anything else?" she asked, as though she were numb enough to take whatever could possibly be next.

"Actually, now that you mention it, there is one more thing. You're getting a new dialogue writer."

Bailey's brown eyes popped. "We are?" she said incredulously. Only two months ago, when she had applied for her mortgage, she had asked for a raise and been told there was no room in the budget. Another writer's salary would be four times what she had asked for. "Am I going to have to kill off one of my writers too?" she asked flippantly. She'd always supervised five breakdown writers and five dialogue writers—no more, no less.

"No, you're just going to have an extra one for a while."

She could tell by the tone in his voice that something fishy was going on here. "Who?" she asked.

Sam began straightening the few papers on his desk as though it were a task of immense importance requiring his complete concentration. "I believe her name is Lindsay Stubblefield," he said efficiently. "Yes, that's it. She'll be starting after the first of the year."

Stubblefield. That explained everything. "So what's her background?" Bailey inquired.

"She's graduating this week from Wellesley."

Great, Bailey thought, one of those snooty all-girl schools. "What's her major?"

"French literature."

"French literature?!" Bailey said with a laugh. "Well, won't that come in handy when we move everyone from Fairview to Marseille and start broadcasting from France!" She was geared up to unleash her disapproval on Sam but again realized there was no point. When Stubblefield barked, they all had to jump.

"Why me? Why our little show?"

Sam's eyes rolled back and his eyelids fluttered slightly, as though he were in the first stages of an aneurysm. "She's got a crush on Beauregard."

Bailey's face puckered up until her squinting brown eyes could barely be seen. "Does she know that

Beauregard Buchanan is only a fictional character...and that the real guy who plays him is a total asshole—a gorgeous asshole but an asshole nonetheless...that the reason Beau is Mr. Wonderful and such a heartthrob is because he's a figment of several female imaginations who managed to dream up the perfect guy who always says and does the right thing at the right time?" She leaned in closer and closer to Sam's face with every word.

"And does she also know that the writers, other than me, never *ever* get to go down on the set or even see the actors on the show? Does she know that the actors look down on the writers as pond scum—no, wait," she said, looking around the cosmos for inspiration, "what's lower than pond scum on the food chain? That they look at us as *plankton?*" she said, glaring at Sam, nose-to-nose. "Does she know that she's going to be reduced to a tiny fleck of plankton, Sam?" she asked, holding up her thumb and index finger a hair's width apart, peering at him through the tiny slit.

The executive just shrugged. "I guess she'll find out when you tell her."

Bailey had visions of having to constantly yank the leash on this little girl with a bad case of puppy love. "You know, baby-sitters get 10 bucks an hour nowadays...am I going to at least see *that* increase on my paychecks?" she asked suggestively, reminding him of the raise she had asked for and been denied.

"I'll keep that in mind," he said, genuinely sympathizing with her.

"No, seriously, you know we write story lines six months in advance and scripts three weeks in advance, which means my staff is going to have to undo *months* of work to accommodate killing off Binaca. It's going to require a truckload of overtime, Sam."

"Whatever it takes," he said sincerely. "Corporate okayed this and they know what it means."

Bailey let out a weary sigh. "Please tell me there's nothing else."

"That's it," Sam said with a smile, relieved this battle was over.

"Thanks so much," she replied, her words dripping with venom, "you've really made my day." She yanked her coat off her chair and left.

Bailey sloshed her way back across the street through the dirty gray snow that remained from a three-day-old snowfall, watching her breath fog up as she puffed out choice dialogue that she *knew* would never make it past the censors.

Chapter Two

When Bailey got back to her office, Peter was meticulously spreading their lunch on the conference table at the far end of her office, where the breakdown writers gathered on Tuesdays and Fridays from 10 to 2 to work up plot lines for the show. One white wall was covered top to bottom with six large monthly planners; the other was home to a giant white marking board that served as the current week's storyboard. With so many characters and plot lines going at one time, this was the only way to make sure the wrong people didn't fall into bed with each other.

"I hope you don't mind me ordering for you," Peter said as he placed Bailey's food on one of the embroidered jungle place mats he had made for the office gang in an evening crafts class last summer. "I had no idea how long you were going to be held up. I got you a Reuben, just the way you like it—mustard, no sauce—and a side order of coleslaw."

"Thanks, Peter, you're a doll," Bailey said, flopping into her chair.

"So...dish!" he said anxiously as he whipped out a matching jungle napkin and tucked it into the neck of his blue Oxford shirt that was buttoned to the top, despite the fact that he never wore a tie. "What was the big news from Slinky?"

Bailey hit him first with the news about the new addition to the dialogue staff. Then she told him about Binaca. "Christmas on a cracker!" Peter exclaimed. "I'm glad I didn't take a bite of my sandwich yet or I would have choked!" He spent the next five minutes expressing his disdain for the decision to knock off his favorite character.

"So are you going to have to break the news to Morgan?" he asked fearfully.

"Not me," Bailey said with great relief, taking a huge bite of a kosher pickle. "Mike gets that plum assignment. Actually, he won't break it to her directly, he'll call her agent first, then her agent will relay the message. I tell you, the protocol in the entertainment business is ridiculous. No one ever talks to anyone face-to-face."

Peter snickered. "Like the time Derek went to Stubblefield refusing to do that Viagra story line we wrote a couple years back."

Bailey almost spit out her food, she laughed so hard. "He was so afraid it would tarnish his macho image," she said, shaking her head. "I guess he thought people were going to think it was really *him* having a bout of Limp Dick Syndrome and not his character. Men," she said with exasperation.

"I remember Stubblefield's secretary saying Derek went absolutely ballistic, ranting and raving like a maniac about how he would quit the show before he'd do that bit," Peter said.

"What a baby," Bailey replied, her face in a snarl.

Peter raised an eyebrow as he poked at his cup of coleslaw with a plastic fork. "Methinks the man doth protest too much," he said in crisp syllables.

Bailey stopped chewing. "What?"

He pursed his lips. "I think we may have accidentally hit closer to home than we realized," he said confidentially.

Bailey grinned. "Oh, really?" she replied, interested in hearing more.

Peter quickly scooted his chair closer. "I heard through the grapevine that Derek hadn't had a date in months before that story line came up, which is odd for Derek—you know how he's constantly bragging about which starlet he's banging. And then, one night the cleaning crew found a bunch of articles about Viagra that had been cut out of newspapers and magazines in his trash can. They'd been stuffed down to the bottom so no one would see them, but then, of course, when the crew dumped them, all the stuff at the bottom was on the top."

"Uh-oh!" she giggled. "Well, that would certainly explain things, wouldn't it?"

"It would indeed."

Bailey chomped on the last bit of her pickle. "Apparently he has no balls, either, because he didn't even come talk to me himself—he had to go right to

Stubblefield! He should have come to me, and if not me, then Mike, and if he couldn't talk to Mike, then it should have been Sam, then as a last resort, Stubblefield. Talk about skipping a few steps."

She paused to wash her food down with a healthy chug of Coke. "It's such an impersonal business," she continued. "That's one reason I liked Morgan so much," she said with a touch of sadness. "She actually came up and talked to me like a person." Then she shrugged it off. "Oh, well."

Suddenly a shadowy figure appeared in the doorway and knocked on the open door, making both writers jump. It was Morgan Gable. Bailey and Peter looked at each other, relieved they hadn't been busted by Derek but worried Morgan may have overheard their gossip.

The busty, raven-haired actress came charging in, full of her trademark headstrong energy. Although she was a petite package, there was nothing meek or mild about Morgan Gable. She was fully made-up for the day's shoot and still had the white tissues tucked into the neckline of her Chanel suit jacket. "Well, kids," she said exuberantly, "I got the bad news this morning." She looked skyward and sighed melodramatically. "And I was just starting to like Fairview," she pined, then quickly scowled. "Except for Ace Atkinson...I guess he just couldn't stand the competition, huh?"

The two writers got the double entendre, but they also knew Morgan really meant she was starting to like the people associated with the show and now those ties of affection were going to be severed, which was a constant but difficult part of an actor's life. Bailey and

Peter couldn't help feeling a little sorry for her.

"So, I wanted to come up and tell you that since I've got to go, all I ask is that you send me out with a bang!" the actress said with a dramatic flourish of an arm. Then she stepped behind Bailey and cradled each of the writer's strong shoulders in her hands. "I think I'll miss you most of all, Scarecrow," she said sweetly, then patted Bailey on one shoulder.

The writers took a few minutes to express their sorrow to Morgan, which the actress genuinely appreciated. "Ah, well, 'tis the nature of our business," she said wistfully, then departed to the set.

Suddenly the task that lay before them hit Peter. "Jesus, does this mean we're all going to be putting in a lot of overtime right at the holidays?" he fussed, then picked up his plastic cup of coleslaw again to finish it off.

Bailey shook her head. "I'll do most of it myself for the next couple of weeks. I know everyone wants to be with their families around Christmas."

"That's a nice gesture, but won't Miranda feel neglected with you spending so much time at the office?" He focused on his food while waiting for a response to his question. When none came, he looked over at Bailey. Her hands were cradled in her lap and her face was all screwed up. At first he thought she was choking, but then he realized she was crying. First it was a tiny trickle from her eyes, then the dam burst and the tears flowed. "She broke up with me!" Bailey wailed loudly.

Peter immediately put down his food and scooted

over to give his friend a hug. Even though Bailey was his boss, the two were good friends, and he and his partner, Alec, had socialized with Bailey at least once a month in the four years he'd been with the show. "Oh, Bailey, I'm so sorry. When did this happen?" He handed her a clean paper napkin to dry her tears.

"Last night," she said, dabbing her eyes. "We went out to dinner and she was acting weird and snippy all night, then we went to my place to watch a movie and I tried to kiss her and she pulled back and—" The tears came pouring again, leaving her unable to continue.

"What in the world happened?"

Bailey sat very quiet for a moment, then her face contorted painfully. "She's in love with someone else," she groaned, as though the words hurt just as much as the deed.

"Oh, no," Peter said sorrowfully.

"She's been seeing someone else for the last *two months!*" she shouted, then blew her nose.

Peter took in a gasp. "I don't believe it!" Bailey nodded in affirmation of her statement. "And you didn't know? Wait—what am I saying?" he said, raising his hands in the air. "Of course you didn't know—obviously you didn't know!"

"So we got in a big fight—she finally stormed out around 2 o'clock. Then she came back at the crack of dawn on her way to work to pick up her toothbrush and the things she kept at my place for nights she stayed over, and we picked up where we left off last night."

Bailey sniffled into the soggy napkin again. "She

cleaned out her drawer, Peter," she whined, then started sobbing hard. "Her little drawer in my dresser that I gave her to keep her things in...and now it's empty!" she bawled, her strong shoulders shaking like two Jell-O molds.

Something about the way Bailey was sitting, her slumped posture, the brokenhearted expression—she just looked so helpless in Peter's eyes...like a child who had lost something precious and didn't know who to turn to for help. He squeezed her tight. "Poor baby. You've just had a bad day right from the start, haven't you? Is there anything I can do?"

Bailey looked up with pleading puppy-dog eyes. "You could come over for dinner tonight so I don't have to spend this first night all alone."

"Oh, I wish I could, but Alec's girls are in their school Christmas play tonight and you-know-who will be there," he snarled, referring to Alec's ex-wife, whom the architect had married ages ago when he was still in the closet—or as Peter referred to it, still vacationing in Heteroland. "You know how these family things are," he said, sounding perturbed.

Bailey didn't know, but she said she understood. "That's all right...I'll be okay," she said, putting on a brave front. "After all, I have the girls to keep me company."

Peter knew she was referring to the three stray cats she had rescued from the mean streets of New York over the years. She considered them her children, doting on them whenever they were sick, getting each one Christmas presents every year and their own tiny red stocking to hang on the mantle. Bailey loved her kitties, and Peter knew the love of a cat might suffice for tonight, but what about tomorrow and the next night, when the loneliness really started to sink in?

"You are still coming to the Christmas party this Saturday night, aren't you?" he said, referring to the annual cast and crew party, hoping it would give his friend something to look forward to.

"I don't feel much like celebrating, Peter. I think I'll pass this year."

"Oh, come on," he said encouragingly, "I can fix you up with a date, if you want."

Bailey recoiled. "It's a little soon, but thanks anyway."

"Okay, then how about someone to just partner up with for the evening?" he asked, trying to take the pressure off a little.

"Thanks, but no," she replied. "I don't think I'm going to even go."

He gave her a knowing look. "Everyone will ask where you are and rumors will go *fly-ing*," he said, singing the last word. She knew that was true too. Biggest bunch of vicious gossips she'd ever seen in this extended family. "Plus we've already drawn secret Santa names, and if you don't show up, someone will be without a present." He pooched out his bottom lip like a disappointed baby, and the silly face was enough to make Bailey smile again.

"Oh, all right," she said, "I'll make an appearance."

He smiled too and patted her on the back. "Good! You'll have a great time—you wait and see. And as far as that other matter goes, I'll give you *one month* to recover, then I'm going to fix you up with Ms. Right," he said, giving her a friendly wink, then started setting up the television for her daily 2 o'clock viewing of the broadcast.

❧

That night, Bailey sat eating take-out ravioli directly from the carton in her darkened living room, which was bathed in golden sepia tones from the flames of a toasty fire and the gentle glow of Christmas lights on her tree. She hadn't been in the mood to cook a meal for just herself, so she settled for dinner to go, which she didn't even have the incentive to put on a plate. All her children—Puddin, Bosco, and Punkin—were curled up and cuddled up on the sofa with her, sleeping off their dinner in the warmth of the fire.

Bailey kicked up her feet on the coffee table and accidentally knocked over the empty plastic container of yogurt encrusted with remnants from this morning's breakfast—her dishes and glass still where she'd left them hours ago. She had intended to clean the house that evening but hadn't been able to muster up enough energy to straighten her small apartment: two decent-size bedrooms, a formal living and dining room. The simple task felt too overwhelming tonight. So what if she left her breakfast things on the table for another day—no one was going to see them...not now. She sniffled, trying to hold back the tears, but she didn't have the strength to accomplish that either.

The sounds of Bailey boo-hooing spooked Punkin and she jumped onto the coffee table, knocking over the nearly empty juice glass, causing it to shatter. Dregs of orange juice seeped over the tabletop. "Oh, *Punkin!*" Bailey shouted, then picked up the empty yogurt cup and threw it at the orange-and-white cat, causing her to leap halfway across the room and jet down the dark hall to safety. Bailey glared at the mess. Now she *had* to clean things up.

After finishing her chore, Bailey flopped onto the couch, limp as a Raggedy Ann doll, and sat for a few minutes looking out the picture window at Central Park. It looked so pretty with the blanket of snow still white and clean, the empty branches of all the trees frosted with white. This was what had sold her on buying the apartment—this view. The unit was pricey for its size, but the window framed a spectacular view of Mother Nature's beauty that she couldn't pass up. There was something so peaceful about the park, no matter what time of year it was. And tonight she needed that peace and tranquillity.

Minutes later she noticed Punkin at the entrance to the living room, timidly poking her head in to see whether it was safe to reenter. Bailey called to the cat in loving tones a few times until the feline pranced over to her ankles and began rubbing against her legs, back and forth, tail quivering. Bailey picked up her cat and hugged it for a long time, stroking its fur affectionately. "I'm sorry,

Punkin," she said softly just before she broke down into tears again. "I shouldn't be taking it out on you...you guys are all I've got left."

She gathered her brood next to her for comfort while she cried out her misery and loneliness in the still of the winter's night.

Chapter Three

Life behind the scenes of a soap opera can be every bit as chaotic and weird as the show itself. With myriad plot lines and characters weaving their way through Fairview, the potential existed for all sorts of mishaps. The show's bizarre writing and shooting schedules didn't help matters any.

On Tuesdays and Fridays from 10 to 2, Bailey met with Peter and the four other breakdown writers in her office to churn out five days of plot lines, working six months in advance. From 3 to 6 on those days, and all day Wednesdays, she and Peter fleshed out those plots. Mondays she spent meeting with the network brass. Meanwhile, the dialogue writers worked under the supervision of Max Patterson, except on Thursdays, when Bailey joined them, fine-tuning their completed scripts. After a script was polished and met her approval, she sent it off to S&P to see if it could pass muster.

Three weeks after an idea was hatched, the script was ready to shoot. Once the show was shot, the completed tape was also sent to the censors for viewing, to make sure none of the actors had gotten a wild hair and slipped one in on them. Finally, after a total of six weeks from conception, the show was broadcast.

Because there were a lot of details to keep track of on a soap—especially one with a 30-year history—on occasion something would get overlooked. Like the time Heather Donnelley's character, Aruba Banks—the standard Beautiful Blond Bitch—was in a lunch scene at a restaurant that was shot on a Thursday.

Then, because of the time warp in Soapland in which a day can last for an entire week, the next scene from that same day, when Aruba returns to her office, wasn't shot until the following Tuesday. In the meantime, Heather had gone out over the weekend and gotten hair extensions. So much real time had passed that no one on the set thought anything about it, but when the show aired, it looked as though Aruba's hair had grown a foot on the drive back to the office from lunch. Little things like that could really creep up and bite you on the ass.

Fortunately for Bailey, mistakes like that weren't her responsibility—that fell under the jurisdiction of Doris Collingsworth, the continuity person for the show. However, there were plenty of mines out there for the writing staff to wend their way through, and since there were no reruns, which meant no days off, Bailey and the writers were in a continuous state of frazzle...which didn't make it any easier to break the bad news to her writers on Tuesday about killing off Binaca.

She explained to the group that the situation wouldn't affect the dialogue writers because they worked only three weeks ahead; the show could afford to wait that long to start working in changes that would eventually lead up to a spectacular demise for their villain. But for the breakdown writers, this meant months of hard work had just gone spiraling down the proverbial crapper.

≈

While Bailey was upstairs dealing with the group of suicidal writers, downstairs on the set the 10 o'clock rehearsal of the day's show was in progress. The morning blocking rehearsal wasn't so much for the actors to make sure they knew their lines, but to coordinate the timing, camera angles, lighting, et cetera, so the taping at 2 o'clock would go smooth as silk. It was a chance to get the bugs out so they didn't waste time and money on the real thing.

On this particular morning the set was abuzz as usual, with dozens of actors and crew scattered about. The 10 fully furnished sets—constructed much like a huge furniture warehouse showroom—were split in two by a wide span of floor space, which was necessary for the three cameras to have room to maneuver.

All the young femmes fatales had draped themselves over beds and sofas on the sets that wouldn't be used that day, yawning and stretching, trying to wake up, looking much like the felines that had taken over the Hemingway House in Key West. They looked grungy and unglamorous in their curlers and no make-up, wearing baggy warm-ups and dirty sneakers. The men, however, all looked gorgeous, even without makeup and hair. As one actress had put it on her first day on the set, "It's a curse...life is so unfair."

During the run-through of the first scene in Binaca's office at *The Tribune,* the show's director, Blaine Edwards, tired of the distracting chatter in the background and yelled for quiet. But everyone gave him the Rodney Dangerfield treatment, and the low buzz filling the floor continued. Blaine moved the eight actors in the scene around like human chess pieces until he got them positioned just the way he wanted, then started the scene again.

In the middle of a heated argument between Binaca and Fairview's hospital administrator, Sloan Kettering, the painted backdrop of the downtown skyline outside her office window suddenly started to wobble. "Are we having an earthquake today—is that in the script?" Blaine shouted, then looked toward Marci, the script girl, who immediately began checking the pages of the day's script spread out on the moveable podium where she and Blaine camped out.

A crew member in fraying jeans, a flannel shirt, and a green John Deere cap shyly stepped out from behind the noisy backdrop. "Sorry," he said, blushing with embarrassment, then tiptoed off as well as he could in a pair of heavy black workman's boots. The actors tried hard not to laugh, but Blaine didn't find it the least bit funny and instructed the actors to start the scene once more.

Twenty minutes later the action shifted to the other side of the floor, to the living room set of Priscilla Barnaby and her evil twin sister, Drucilla—both of whom had been played by Kerri Summers for the last two months. "What's your name today?" someone shouted with a laugh. "I don't know," the sleepy actress said, propping herself up on the back of a soft upholstered chair, "ask me after lunch."

Priscilla delivered her speech flawlessly, then the director shouted, "Cue Bruschetta!" But the actress who played Bruschetta, the family's Italian cook, was deep in conversation with several women on the set across the floor and didn't hear him. One of the women she was talking with slapped her on the shoulder and gave her the hitchhikers' thumb, meaning "hit the road—you're up," and away she sprinted, coming to a bone-jarring halt next to Priscilla before spewing out her line: "Yes, madam—you called?"

"Just e-e-e-ver so slightly behind cue," Blaine said, making everyone crack up. "Let's try it again with Bruschetta a little closer this time." He pointed to the space on the floor next to him, meaning for her to stand there until her cue.

For the next scene, the action hastily shifted to the country club set, where a bridal shower was to be held. During the entire scene, there was a continual rumble from above, as someone was rather noisily adjusting the large bank of lights overhead, causing the sides of their metal housing to warble periodically. "Are we having thunder *inside* the country club?" Blaine snapped. The heavy-metal thunder immediately ceased.

The scene's climax involved a verbal catfight between Aruba and Pashmina Shaw—the latter the bride-to-be, whose fiancé, Beau Buchanan, had once been in love with Aruba. Of late, Aruba had been desperately trying to seduce Beau and win him back. And after perfectly spouting off a grand tirade in which she threatened to take Beau away from Pashmina before the wedding could occur, Aruba picked up her prop purse, preparing for a dramatic exit, and said with great smarm, "Say Beau to hi for me!" Everyone roared with laughter. "Aw, *damn* it!" Heather cried out, stomping her feet and squealing in disgust as everyone applauded her faux pas.

While the guests at the bridal shower filed out of the country club, one woman took a leaf up the nose from a robust potted ficus at the entrance. "This really doesn't work here, does it?" she said, laughing at herself as she vigorously rubbed the tickle from her nose. The bushy tree was efficiently removed from the set by two set decorators.

By noon the rehearsal was over and the actors adjourned for a quick lunch in order to be back in "the chair" by 1 for an hour of makeup and hair before the taping at 2 o'clock sharp.

❧

Back upstairs, Bailey and the breakdown writers were in full swing trying to come up with some new story lines. "We need to rework this scene with Rambo and RuWanda after she regains her sight," Bailey instructed. "What can we have him do to terrorize her?"

Deirdre said, "How about kidnapping her illegitimate daughter, Mocha Latte? That's pretty dramatic." Deirdre sounded proud of her idea until she noticed LeeAnn frowning. "You don't like my suggestion?" she asked.

"That's not it," LeeAnn replied listlessly. "I was just hoping we could maybe write out this Rambo character, since we're doing a lot of serious rearranging."

Everyone seemed surprised she wanted to get rid of the hot young psycho killer they had created only a year ago; he'd been on the cover of all the soap magazines several times since his debut. "What's your problem with Rambo?" Evan asked.

"Well, you know he was originally supposed to be only a day-character. That's why I named him after my uncle, Roger Rambo."

"Yeah, I remember," Evan said, "which is why I'm surprised to hear you want to give him the ax."

"Well, I suggested my uncle's name because I thought my family would get a kick out of having a character on TV who's named after a family member. But over the last several months, Rambo's turned into such a slimy scuzzbucket that Uncle Roger and half the family hate me now because they think I was insulting him, like I didn't like him or something. You have *no idea* what hell my life is now," she said wearily, "and with the holidays coming up and all those *cozy* family gatherings..." She looked at Bailey with pleading eyes. "Help me!" she cried, her arms outstretched in a dramatic breakdown worthy of any character in Fairview.

Bailey laughed sympathetically. "Sorry, the network just picked up his option for another year."

"Oh, God," LeeAnn groaned, putting her head down on the table and covering it with her arms, as if trying to hide from the world. "I was hoping to give them some good news for the holidays. Oh, well," she whined, "I guess I can expect twigs and coal in my stocking this year."

＆

The remainder of the writing session was completely unproductive—with their minds bombarded with weeks and weeks of plot lines reversing course, everyone was stumbling over themselves trying to sort things out. Bailey was glad when 2 o'clock finally rolled around so she could send them all home and let her brain rest.

She closed the door to her office, which indicated to her secretary, Wanda, that she did not want to be disturbed. Then she kicked up her feet and ate lunch alone while she watched the show.

Bailey always enjoyed this hour of quiet, seeing the fruits of her labor come to life. Today's show started out in a restaurant scene with Ace and Mink Mansfield, a busty gold-digging stripper who was attracted to the silver-haired millionaire for the obvious reason. In the scene, Mink was smooth-talking him, hoping to get him to buy her a diamond necklace she had seen in a store window. Bailey was just getting into the seduction scene when something distracted her.

Ace's wine glass was nearly full as he was speaking, but she could have sworn the glass had been nearly empty just seconds ago, the last time he was on camera. Sure enough, as the scene intercut—showing Ace from over Mink's shoulder as he spoke, then Mink from the reverse angle as she spoke—Ace's wine glass alternated from full to empty every time he was on camera.

At first Bailey wondered how that detail could have slipped by without anyone on the set noticing. Then she remembered that they'd had to reshoot this scene several days later, because a reflection from one of the mirrors in the restaurant's entrance had washed out half of Derek's face on tape. Apparently the video editors either got the two tapes mixed together or thought some of the original scenes were worth saving. Regardless, it looked hilarious on screen and Bailey laughed out loud.

"Doris is gonna get her butt chewed today!" she shouted gleefully, not because she disliked Doris, but because that dark cloud she had been under yesterday had moved on and was pissing on someone else.

As the music played over the closing credits, Bailey gathered up her things to leave for a dental appointment and was inspired to play announcer: "Tune in tomorrow, same time, same station, as we continue airing the dirty laundry of Fairview in the continuing saga of *All the Bold Days of My Restless Life.*" She turned out the lights and closed the door behind her.

≥•

The annual Christmas party at the studio was in full swing by 9 o'clock Saturday night. This was the one day of the year when all the lowly union members and all the lofty guild members came together as equals—thanks to the wonders of alcohol. Everyone was dressed in holiday colors, the women in formal gowns and cocktail dresses. Bailey had gone all out and worn her black tuxedo, accessorized by a red-and-green plaid cummerbund.

This year's theme was *White Christmas,* and the set designers had transformed the open floor area into the final scene of the movie, where the gigantic sliding doors of the white wooden ski lodge are opened for all the guests to glimpse the long-awaited holiday snow—which was provided by three large mechanical rocking bins made of chicken wire and filled with Styrofoam flakes that came floating gently down from the heavens.

Christmas carols and seasonal songs provided a cozy, festive atmosphere while people danced and talked. Several rectangular tables had been pushed together in the middle of the floor, making one long dining table that was covered by red linen tablecloths sporting white garlands scalloped along the edges. Each of the 80 place settings was complete with

Wedgwood china, a half-dozen silver utensils, and three stems of crystal for a multicourse dinner. The party was always catered by one of the five-star hotels in the city, and this night's menu included caviar appetizers, artichoke and hearts of palm salad with a lime vinaigrette dressing, filet mignon with porcini mushroom sauce and lyonnaise potatoes as the entrée, and for dessert, a grand chocolate-raspberry torte covered with chocolate leaves and fresh red raspberries.

Dinner would be served at 9:30; until then, there was plenty of champagne and a large crystal punch bowl filled with rich, golden eggnog to keep the conversation flowing—which seemed to be working. Everyone was getting lit quicker than a Christmas candle.

Derek was about 80-proof by this time and on his fifth glass of champagne. He had just begun regaling Bailey, Peter and Alec, and a dozen others with an intense review of a movie he'd rented the night before that had fascinated him to the point of obsession. He had gone on and on about it for almost five minutes before someone finally grew curious enough to ask the name of the film. "Damn it, I can't remember...but you know which one I'm talking about...the one about the slutty lap dancers...the one with all the hype that said it was going to be the smash hit of the decade." He rubbed his temple to stimulate his brain. "*Callgirls!*" he said, snapping his fingers.

"*Showgirls,*" someone corrected, but to no avail— Derek's pickled ears didn't pick up the word.

"It starred the most luscious girl I've seen in

ages...oh, what was her name? She played on one of those high school TV shows before she turned into a movie slut...Busby Berkeley!"

After a moment someone said, "Elizabeth Berkley."

"Ah, it was a masterpiece of shit written by that guy who wrote *Basic Instinct*—now don't tell me...I *know* this name...Joe Everhazy!" he announced confidently, almost boasting.

"Joe Eszterhas," one of the guys offered.

Derek looked at the man who had just corrected him like he was an idiot. "That's what I said," he replied, sounding indignantly inebriated. "My God, that man writes filthy movies...you should have seen these young, round women writhing on those poles...and this Berkley girl takes her tongue and licks that pole from top to bottom...a-a-a-h," he groaned lustily. "God, I would *love* to have been that pole," he added, which totally creeped everyone out.

"I'll bet," Peter said under his breath, giving Bailey a knowing glance.

She jabbed Peter in the ribs, then got the hell out of there just in case his words eventually made their way into Derek's brain.

While Bailey milled about talking with her co-workers and their dates, Morgan Gable made a grand entrance that got everyone's attention. The actress was decked out in the famous red velvet Edith Head gown she'd worn in *Fire and Ice,* the romantic drama that had made her a sex symbol at the ripe old age of 18, in no small part due to her fabulous and now legendary D-cup bosom. In that movie she seduced her leading man in a sizzling, passionate love scene that set the film world on its ear.

Everyone gathered around, raving about Morgan's dress and how she still looked just as beautiful and sexy in it as she had 45 years ago, when the movie was first released. She, of course, did not tell them that the dress had been let out twice over the decades—once in the waist; once in the rump.

It wasn't long before someone in the crowd shouted out a request for her to sing the title song she had sung in the film. After a little coaxing from dozens more, the CD player was silenced, and Morgan took the floor and began belting out the song without the aid of a microphone.

Her loud, clear voice burst into song so abruptly it caused Derek to slosh his drink. "Good Lord!" he cried, trying to brush the drops of champagne off his lapel before they soaked in. "All right," he groused as he looked around disgustedly, "who brought the basset hound?"

Some laughed instinctively, then immediately covered their mouths, but most who heard the remark were shocked and looked directly at Morgan to see how she would react. She had heard the insult, but being a professional, didn't miss a beat.

As she listened, Bailey became mesmerized by the actress. Those deep, Mediterranean-blue cat eyes fringed with thick jet-black lashes; her raven hair and eyebrows, which contrasted with her creamy, smooth skin. Bailey remembered—from her own days as a young girl—the sweetness of Morgan in her younger days, so different from today's ingenues, with their whorish makeup, bare midriffs, navel rings, and silicone bags shoved in our faces. Bailey remembered clearly the unfathomable allure Morgan Gable possessed—the pretty girl with the sweet smile, but with the body of a woman and eyes that revealed only a hint of the sensual, sexual creature within.

And like the blue Mediterranean waters, beneath the surface one found the intrigue of hidden depths. It was that aura of mystery surrounding Morgan that people had been drawn to and enveloped by. And she still had it. "You know," Bailey sighed, "it's easy to understand why she was once known as the most beautiful woman in the world. God, she's still so pretty."

Derek snorted. "I never could look at her that long myself...especially with that mole of Iglesian proportion on her upper lip. Look at it, just hanging there like a big booger," he said with a shudder.

Bailey, Peter, and Alec exchanged a quick glance. Derek's reference to Morgan's tiny beauty mark was obviously just his jealousy talking.

Derek sipped his champagne as he watched the performance, then scowled. "Someone give the woman a tissue!" he said, turning away as if he might throw up at any second.

The actress finished the song like a trouper and received thunderous applause for the unrehearsed performance. She placed her hands on her hips and immodestly said, "I still got the chops."

"Yes," Derek said haughtily from the periphery, "for a moment I thought Ethel Merman had come back and joined us." He made a face and threw back the rest of his champagne as if it were a medical necessity. Morgan sent a couple of daggers flying in his direction, which only bounced off the man as he walked away.

&

The grand dinner was finished by 11, at which time Santa Claus made an appearance and distributed all the secret Santa gifts from the giant red sack slung over his shoulder. It was standard procedure that all gifts were to be gag gifts, but they also were supposed to be tailored to the person—or in the case of the actors, to the character they played. The gift opening would begin at one end of the table and go down the line, each person standing to open his or her gift so everyone could see.

This year the first to open his gift was Joe Martinelli, the tall, dark, muscular actor who played Blaze Blizzard, Fairview's hot vice squad cop with the icy exterior. Once the wrapping paper was discarded, he opened the thin box and pulled out a black lace garter belt. Everyone hooted and hollered, knowing this was a token reminder of the show a few weeks ago when Blaze had gone undercover dressed like a hooker to catch Rambo, the serial killer. To look at Joe, one wouldn't think such a big, strong guy would be so shy, but he had been raised in Nebraska with Midwestern values, and that scene had been exceptionally difficult for him to get through. "Put it on!" someone shouted, causing him to blush like a schoolgirl and quickly sit down.

After several more gifts were opened, it was Heather's turn. Her gift was a Juiceman—a fruit and vegetable juicer, given in fond remembrance of her kissing scene with one incredibly slobbery day-character they all later referred to as the Juice Man. "That guy is the answer to California's water shortage," she groaned at the disgusting memory. But even Heather had to laugh at the clever gift idea.

While the evening wore on, Derek, who was sitting at the far end of the table nursing his eighth glass of champagne, had grown inordinately fascinated with his small gift—a thin, five-inch square wrapped in shiny gold paper with a small red bow in the center. He knew it was customary to wait his turn, but there were a dozen people ahead of him. Soon curiosity got the best of him and he became like the child on Christmas morning who wanted to be the first down to the tree—he simply couldn't wait any longer.

Turning sideways in his chair, he put his back to the crowd that was focused on Mitch Carrington, the actor who played Beauregard, and with restrained glee Derek quickly tore away the crisp golden paper.

Suddenly his eyes bulged and a chill of horror rushed through him. He was holding a CD titled *Limp Bizkit.*

His head sprang back around, eyes darting from face to face, hoping no one had seen. All eyes were still on Mitch and the commotion surrounding him, so

Derek shoved the plastic square into his jacket like a criminal concealing a gat in a '40s gangster movie, his shifty eyes making absolutely certain he had not been detected.

Who on earth knew? He hadn't told *anyone*—not his doctor, not his best friend, none of the women he had dated—no one. But this couldn't be a coincidence. Someone knew.

He slipped out of his chair and zigzagged across the floor, taking refuge behind one set, then another, like Fagin skulking though the dingy streets of Dickensian London with his loot stashed beneath his tattered coat. He slipped behind one of the prop doors of the makeshift ski lodge at the end of the soundstage while squinting eyes sifted carefully through the falling flakes of Styrofoam snow, scrutinizing those gathered just one more time for the slightest hint of recognition in the face of his tormentor. But all were engaged in conversation, or food, or Peter, who was now opening his gift. Apparently no one had even noticed Derek's departure. Yet someone, somewhere in this room had discovered his dirty little secret.

One by one, he scanned the faces of those seated at the table, when suddenly his eyes locked with a pair of ice-cold blue eyes that sparkled with the fire of mischief and vindictiveness. Morgan Gable was sitting across from Joe Martinelli at the far end of the table, resting her chin on her left hand, which held one of the slim cigars she had developed such a fondness for over the years. The cigar, which had been resting at an erect angle, suddenly drooped. A

Grinchly grin crept across her face.

Derek sucked in an audible gasp that put white caps on the East River. Mother of God! Why did it have to be Morgan?! He charged toward the exit, mortified by thoughts of what this she-wolf intended on doing next to torture him.

Chapter Four

On Tuesday, the first morning back after the New Year's break, Wanda arrived carrying a steaming cup of Starbucks coffee and a cheese Danish in her bare hands—one hand stinging from the cold, the other from the scalding coffee that had sloshed out from under the lid. She set them on her desk and shivered as she flung her coat on top of one of the chairs used for waiting visitors. Only then did she notice the young, pretty blond standing beside her desk looking at a scribbled note she was holding.

The girl was tall and a little bony, straight hair down to her waist, and she was dressed like a parochial schoolgirl in a plaid wool skirt with a white oxford shirt, cotton kneesocks, and penny loafers. "Can I help you?" Wanda asked in her thick Brooklyn accent.

The girl looked at the secretary, then at the room number above Bailey's office door. "I was told Bailey Connors's office was Room 200," she said, her brow furrowed.

"It is," Wanda snapped, licking the white icing off her fingers.

"Well, when I peeked my head in just now, the only person in there was a guy sitting behind the desk. He looked pretty comfortable."

Wanda smiled. "That's probably Peter—he's Bailey's senior writer. Sometimes he sits at her desk when she's not around, but this is her office."

"Oh, thanks," the blond said, but instead of taking a seat and waiting for Bailey to arrive, she went right on into the office. Wanda instinctively stood up to stop the stranger, but she was starving and dying to dig into the Danish. And since the girl was wearing the appropriate badge from the security desk downstairs, Wanda figured she was cleared to be up here, so what the hell—Peter could take care of her until Bailey arrived.

The stranger walked straight up to the desk with her hand extended. "Hi, you must be Peter. I'm Lindsay Stubblefield. I wasn't sure this was Bailey Connors's office at first," she said, explaining her reappearance.

"It is," came the reply, "and *I'm* Bailey Connors."

Lindsay stopped short and slowly lowered her hand. The voice was definitely feminine, but lordy, the scowling face looking up at her was not. Surely this was a mistake a lot of people must have made, because this woman totally looked like a man. "I'm so sorry!" she exclaimed. "I...I..."

Bailey quickly ushered the stammering girl back to the door and opened it. "Why don't you go into the break room and wait for Max and the others," she said, pointing to the room down the hall. "You'll be working with them, and you're a little early."

"I know," Lindsay gushed proudly with a blinding smile, clasping her hands together with excitement. "It's my first day, and I wanted to make a good impression." She bounced down the hall toward the break room, her long hair swinging back and forth with each step.

Bailey stood, her mouth agape, watching Marsha Brady walk away. A good impression. Indeed.

⚜

It wasn't until two days later that Bailey encountered Lindsay again, at her weekly Thursday session with the dialogue writers. However, the head writer already had been informed by a couple people from the dialogue group that Lindsay had not made a good first impression on them either.

For a college grad, they concluded, Lindsay was a little dense. And this being her first job, she couldn't seem to understand the concept of the corporate two-week vacation policy, office politics, or paying one's dues before getting perks. Seems that on her very first day at work she had finagled Max into giving her a week and a half off at the end of January, because she had already arranged to go on a ski vacation in Aspen with her sorority sisters. When Bailey caught wind of this, however, she insisted Max inform Lindsay that, like the rest of them, she would not be able to take two weeks off until after she'd been there a year.

It was apparent to everyone that this child had been born and raised in the protective bubble of money and affluence, and her personality simply didn't mesh with the rest of the staff—most of whom had been born and raised in the Bronx, Brooklyn, and Long Island, and all of whom had a good deal of meaningful life experience under their belts. No one was surprised by the clash. After all, back in the late '70s Lindsay's father had been head of daytime programming at the network, making a seven-figure salary, when he met and married the famous Russian supermodel, Babushka, who in her prime made Anna Kournikova look like kreplach. Lindsay had inherited her mother's blond hair, blue eyes, and flawless complexion, plus the ability to wrap men around her finger with little effort.

While the rest of the staff had grown up fending for themselves in the tough boroughs of New York City, Lindsay Stubblefield had been comfortably ensconced in private boarding schools in Switzerland since the age of 12, when her parents divorced. Babushka left the States after the split and wanted her daughter closer to her when she moved back to Paris in a fairly successful effort to rekindle her modeling career. So it was no wonder this square peg was having trouble fitting into a round hole. The fact that she was at least 10 years younger than everyone else on the staff didn't help either.

All this explained why Bailey slammed into the wall of tension that filled Max's office when she came in that Thursday morning, just ahead of Lindsay, who entered in a huff and plopped into her chair as though she'd just been sentenced to detention. "Would someone please explain to me what the deal is with this Elvis character?" she groused.

"What do you mean?" Stephano asked.

"Well, every year at this time, his face is plastered all over the TV and newspapers, and thousands of people make a pilgrimage to some podunk place in Tennessee called Graceland!"

"That's because his birthday is January 8," Phillip explained.

"I know, but he's *dead*!"

The others realized Elvis had died a few years before Lindsay had even been born, but, really—to be so dense about The King? "Yes," Stephano said, "but he was the greatest entertainer in the world while he was alive."

"Why?" she practically shouted, with arms opened wide, "because he made a bunch of B movies with big-busted starlets and was some Las Vegas lounge lizard? I don't get it."

The two men gave up and let someone else have a swing at it. Bailey stepped up to the plate. "Elvis Presley changed the world of music and the world itself, to a degree," she said, sounding like a college professor imparting historically significant knowledge upon a student. "His musical style and his performance broke down the walls of sexual oppression that had prevailed until after World War II."

"If you say so."

Bailey suddenly grinned like the cat that ate the

canary and spoke to the others. "You know, my parents went to one of his early concerts, and thank God they had their movie camera with them."

Suzette gasped. "You don't mean?!"

"Yes, ma'am. I have Elvis on film."

Lindsay rolled her eyes. "Well, could you bring the video in someday, 'cause I'd like to see what the big deal is all about."

"No, I can't—since this was before video, it's not like plugging a cassette into a VCR. My parents never got the film transferred to video because they were afraid the photo clerks would steal it." Half the people at the table fully admitted they would have too, if they were the clerk.

"Before video?" the girl said, looking completely lost. "What was that?" Then she snapped her fingers. "Oh—wait...I remember something about this in one of my media classes a couple of semesters ago...is it one of those kinetoscope things?"

The rest of the group recoiled. They had all paid attention in college and knew the kinetoscope was one of Edison's inventions from the 1890s.

"No, actually it's on 8-millimeter film," Bailey explained.

"Ee-u-u-u-ww!" Lindsay cried, her nose crinkling in disgust. "You mean...like *porn* films? Like that Oliver Wendell Holmes guy with the giant schlong?"

Before anyone could recover from the shock to respond, Lindsay jumped up and grabbed her monogrammed leather carryall. "Oh, I forgot to put my lunch in the fridge—I'll be right back."

While everyone tried not to laugh, Stephano looked Bailey square in the eye. "So tell us, do you think talkies are going to ruin the movie industry?" Bailey was still too stunned to respond.

When Lindsay returned, Bailey announced enthusiastically, "The breakdown group finally came up with a story line for Binaca's demise, so we're going to have to start working it into the show immediately. The first thing we need to do today is dump Mink Mansfield."

Phillip looked disappointed. "A-w-w-w, what happened to Mink?"

"She wins $2 million on a slot machine in Vegas when Ace takes her there for a newspaper publishers convention. So actually, she dumps Ace and runs off with his muscular Scottish gardener, Brigadoon."

"Well, that was generous of you," Rhonda said.

"And it's right after that when Ace and Binaca first start becoming interested in each other," Bailey continued. "She consoles him in his loss, and a spark is ignited."

"Really?" Rhonda said. Everyone knew how viciously Derek and Morgan despised each other. "So where is this Ace-Binaca thing going?"

"They have a whirlwind romance and get married on her last show."

Lindsay bounded back into the room just in time to hear Bailey's remark. "O-o-o-h! A wedding!" she said dreamily, clasping her hands to her heart. "I *love* weddings—all the pretty flowers, and everyone getting all dressed up."

But the other two female writers were shocked.

"You're going to knock off the woman at her own wedding?" Suzette said. "That's cold."

"It's not like she hasn't had plenty of 'em before," Stephano quipped, referring to Morgan's six-pack of failed marriages.

"One of my sorority sisters actually got married in Vegas," Lindsay interjected, off in some white-meringue Vera Wang dream. "It was outside in her parents' backyard on this fabulous, colorful patio they'd just put in—it was the prettiest color and it contrasted so well with all the green landscaping and flowering plants. It was done all in those...oh, you know," she said, trying hard to think of the right word, "all those brick-colored bricks," she said with a casual flip of her hand.

Looks of dumbfoundment bounced back and forth across the table without Lindsay picking up on a single one of them. "You mean *terra-cotta*?" Suzette suggested.

Now that her brain had been asked to actually engage, the blond snapped out of it. "Oh...yeah, I guess so," she said with a shrug.

Total silence.

"So," Phillip said, turning to Bailey, "how's Binaca gonna bite it?" he asked, full of curiosity.

"I don't know *how* yet, but I've still got plenty of time—I'll come up with something good, don't worry."

The more Phillip thought about the story line, the more he had to laugh. "So what did Morgan say when you told her about her wedding?"

Everyone else was anxious to hear the answer to this question too, but Bailey threw up a wall of resistance.

"Since when does the head writer go to the actors and tell them about upcoming story lines? You know things don't work that way. She'll find out when she gets her script, just like everyone else." The woman was trying to sound bold and brave, but they all knew she was just chicken. And Bailey read that in their faces. "Look, if she has a problem with it—"

"If?!" Stephano said dramatically.

Bailey looked down her nose at him. "*If* she has a problem with it, I'll handle it. I'll simply remind her that she's a professional actor and this is the role she's been hired to play—it's that simple."

"Well," Phillip said as he pulled out his wallet from his back pocket, "in keeping with our Las Vegas theme, anyone want to make a bet on that?" He held up a $20 bill and waved it about.

"Knock it off!" Bailey snapped. "All right, let's get down to work."

⁂

When the group broke at 1 o'clock for lunch, Lindsay retrieved her lunch accoutrements from the refrigerator and began setting up her Martha Stewart traveling sushi tray on the table. Everyone else stood up, giving the girl dirty looks. "Let's eat in the break room today," Stephano said to the old gang. Bailey recognized the chill from the cold shoulder the four were giving the irritating new kid on the block, but she stayed put. She wasn't crazy about the girl either, but felt obligated as head of the group to make the newcomer feel welcome.

"Oh, sorry about the mix-up the other day," Lindsay said in a perky tone to Bailey.

"Don't worry about it," Bailey replied, which caused Max to ask what happened as he joined them, passing the others on their way toward the door. "She thought I was Peter," Bailey said flatly.

The train heading out the door came to a screeching halt. "You know," Stephano said, as though a stroke of genius had just hit him, "it *is* a lot quieter in here." The potential of drama between their boss and the new girl was too good to pass up, so the gang eagerly reclaimed their seats and began spreading their lunch on the table.

"My bad!" Lindsay said, making a guilty face and pushing those padded shoulders of hers up into her earlobes. Then she let out a giggle of embarrassment at her mistake. "I just felt so awful getting off on the wrong foot like that on my first day," she continued.

"Like I said, don't worry about it," Bailey replied as she unwrapped a turkey sandwich.

Lindsay concentrated on opening the miniature bottle of soy sauce as she spoke. "Well, you just hate to offend people you admire, and I really admire you," she said, finally getting the plastic lid open. "I wish I could be more like you, to tell you the truth," she said with complete honesty.

Bailey's ego surged a bit, but the others suspected a heinous act of brownnosing in the first degree was about to be committed. "Really?" the head writer asked. "How so?"

Lindsay sprinkled the brown sauce over one of her California rolls. "Well, I just can't help marveling at women like you who can go out in public and honestly not give a damn what they look like."

Every sound, every movement stopped, and every eye went to the vacuous girl unsheathing her hand-painted wooden chopsticks.

"I couldn't do it," she rambled on as she meticulously positioned the chopsticks between the fingers of her right hand. "It takes me *two hours* to get ready to go somewhere—and that's just for my hair and make-up. So in the morning, when you add on showering and eating breakfast and a few minutes to just wake up, you're talking three hours of prep time, plus a half-hour limo ride. So to get here at 10, I have to get up at *6:30!*" she groaned, picking up the sushi roll with her chopsticks. "You don't know how lucky you are that you don't have to bother with getting all dolled up every day," she said in Bailey's direction just before biting into the chewy delicacy.

No one had moved a muscle during the entire speech. Then, in unison, all eyes shifted to Bailey, whose mouth was hanging open. "I can't remember when I've had such a compliment," she said with a slight frown.

"Well, you just have to admire a woman who can make it on sheer talent alone," Lindsay chirped, then popped the rest of the sushi into her smiling mouth.

Bailey took a couple more bites of her sandwich, then she suddenly began packing up her things. "You know, I think I'm going to eat in my office—I have a few phone calls I really need to make," she said, then quickly disappeared out the door.

Eyes darted back and forth, telegraphing similar thoughts about this idiot child among them who was so completely oblivious to the hostile atmosphere she was creating for herself.

Chapter Five

"*T*runk!"

The dialogue writers all wanted to know what Bailey was talking about when she came into Max's office bellowing this strange greeting the following Thursday.

"Don't ask," she said, looking extremely perturbed, then she dived into the day's business. "Well," Bailey said to begin the meeting, "I have a slight problem with RuWanda's dialogue in the scene where she's reunited with her daughter, Mocha Latte, after the kidnappers set the girl free."

Lindsay looked crushed because that was one of *her* contributions to the script. Max too was surprised and said, "I thought that rang true—it sounded melodramatic and very soapish to me."

Bailey held up an index finger for silence. "Let me read it out loud and see if anyone else can figure out what the problem is." She cleared her throat. "'I never said I was the best mother in the world...give me a little credit, will you. Credit for being someone who tried...to love you the only way she knew how.'"

Rhonda frowned. "That sounds familiar," she said, trying to recall where she might have heard the words before.

Max shrugged. "Yeah, it sounds familiar because it's good soap shtick. So what if another character on the show has said something similar? It was probably eons ago, and how many fans are going to remember...or care? I know it's a little hackneyed, but it'll probably sound great when RuWanda says it in the heat of the moment."

Bailey cocked her head. "You're probably right...because it sounded great when Sally Field said it."

Rhonda slapped the table. *"Soapdish!"* she shouted.

Stephano let out a big Lucy Ricardo "Ee-u-u-u--w!" with his top lip curled up almost to his nose.

Bailey frowned pathetically at Max. "Don't you ever get out?" she chided.

He hung his head in embarrassment. "That's one of my favorite movies," he confessed.

Lindsay's face beamed. "Me too!" she shouted gleefully. "That's why I thought it would be perfect for *our* soap, you know, 'cause it's about a soap opera!"

No one was sure they had actually heard the words right. Bailey pursed her lips to hold back the words she really wanted to say. Instead, she said, "But you can't just take someone else's words and use them in another body of work."

Lindsay's eyes grew big. "Yes, you can—I hear lines of Shakespeare in all sorts of TV shows and movies."

Bailey smiled understandingly. "Well, that's because Shakespeare's work has been around so long it's now in public domain—there's no copyright infringement to be concerned about."

"But in school we're encouraged to use text from lots of current books to back up a hypothesis—I've used parts of books written by Stephen King, Anne Rice, Tom Clancy."

"That's because your teachers won't get sued," Bailey replied, growing a little impatient. "A book report isn't the same as a script for a television show either. A book report isn't for profit—we are. That's what copyright laws are for, so the copyright owner gets compensated whenever that work is used by someone else in a profit-making venture."

"No! You're wrong!" Lindsay stated in all surety, which shocked everyone. "All you have to do is give the original writer a footnote at the end and that keeps it from being plagiarism," she said flippantly.

Bailey folded her hands on the table. "And just how do you propose we do that on our show—we just throw in one of those little pop-up bubbles with the screenwriter's name in it after RuWanda delivers the line? It doesn't work that way in television!" she shouted, having completely lost her patience, her smile now a mass of clenched teeth.

"Well, that's ridiculous!" the girl groused, making it clear by her tone that she thought Bailey was wrong.

"Well, it's *true,*" Bailey blasted back, her teeth grinding just a little behind her smile. The rest in attendance were surprised to see their Harvard-educated head writer sucked into this childish spat.

Lindsay scooted her chair away from the table, loudly grinding the bottom of the legs across the tile floor, causing a shrill screech. "I'm going to the ladies room," she announced, then stomped out defiantly.

After the door closed, Phillip leaned over to Bailey and whispered, "Is that smile fake?"

"Yes," she said, jaws clenched, "but the tears are real." Then she mumbled, "She has the figure and the IQ of a lamppost," which incited comments and criticisms from the others.

"What the hell is wrong with that girl?" Suzette asked in disbelief.

"And *she* graduated from an Ivy League girls' school?" Stephano said.

"I want to see a sheepskin," Phillip demanded.

Max, of course, stood up for Lindsay, saying, "Come on, cut her some slack."

The staff members were surprised by his response, but Bailey was absolutely shocked. "Does the word 'plagiarism' mean anything to you...'cause we *know* it doesn't mean anything to Lindsay," she shouted, pointing to the empty seat.

This set off a barrage of comments and an angry discussion about what sort of legal trouble Lindsay could get the show into pulling stunts like that.

"The girl can't write!" Bailey finally proclaimed 20 minutes later, prompting Max to go on the defensive once more, saying she was doing fine for her second week. "Oh, yeah?" Bailey shouted, "What about that scene where Drucilla is arguing with her new boyfriend, the Russian rap artist Cagey B?"

Max's head tilted and his eyes narrowed. "How do you know it was a scene Lindsay wrote?" he said, sounding a bit cocky, thinking he'd caught Bailey in her own trap.

The head writer's face lit up with insincere animation. "Well, let me read it to you, and you tell me!" She held up the script as if she were about to deliver the State of the Union address. "'So how many women have you slept with...a thousand? So I'm a thousand and one, huh, just like the dalmatians!'"

Spit laughs emitted from around the table. "The girl can't even count!" Bailey yelled. "Unless you think one of your other writers came up with that gem?" she said, gesturing to those around the table, all of whom looked quite insulted that Max might actually try to blame one of them for that tidbit of idiocy.

"How could you overlook garbage like that and send this script to me for approval?" Bailey said in a scolding tone to the group supervisor. Max opened his mouth to defend himself but was saved by a knock at the door from Wanda, who reluctantly poked her head in. "It's Blaine," she said confidentially to Bailey. "He wants to talk to you...*now*," she added with wide eyes.

Bailey walked across the room, picked up the phone, and punched the blinking button. After a quick conversation, she hung up and came back to the table, smirking at Max. "Lolita is down on the set hiding behind a piece of scenery, causing a flash flood from drooling over Mitch...Blaine wants her removed immediately."

From her tone and the look in her eye, Max knew Bailey was instructing him to do the dirty deed. She thought it would be a good lesson for the married Max to see that this child—who was less than half his age and whom he so obviously had a crush on—had a crush of her own on another man. She'd seen how an office triangle could wreck a smooth working situation and thought it best to nip this one in the bud.

When Max returned with his protege, it was obvious Lindsay hadn't enjoy being retrieved; she pouted, her arms folded across her chest. Bailey struggled to regain her professionalism. "Since you don't seem to understand the legal ramifications of plagiarism, and since you don't seem to believe what *I'm* telling you, I'm going to suggest that Max, your direct supervisor, make an appointment for you with the network's legal office so *they* can explain it until you do understand." Neither Max nor Lindsay said a word about the punishment that had been doled out to them.

"In the meantime, let's talk about some of your other dialogue," she said, reopening the script. "In this scene with Pashmina you have Aruba saying, 'My eyes were annoyed.'" She looked over at the girl. "You can't say her eyes were annoyed, because the word 'annoyed' is an emotion and eyes can't have emotions."

"Yes, they can!" Lindsay countered, wondering how this big fat pig ever got a job as a writer. "I read it in books and poetry all the time—she had *yearning* in her eyes, his eyes were filled with *anguish.*"

Bailey shook her head vigorously. "It's not the same thing. Eyes can *reflect* yearning, or *be filled* with anguish, but the eyes, themselves, can't feel these things—you can't say 'my eyes were annoyed.'"

Lindsay looked at the woman like she was an idiot. "Of course you can," she said.

A strong hand slammed the script shut, and Bailey glared at Lindsay with greatly annoyed eyes of her own. "No, you can't! *Annoyed* is a feeling that requires a brain, therefore eyes *cannot* be annoyed, because they don't have a brain!"

In the split second that followed, Bailey's anger and frustration wrestled with her professionalism—quickly pinning the latter to the ground—and instead of holding back the obvious finish to that statement because this was the daughter of the head of daytime programming, the words came barreling out of her mouth. "And apparently neither do you!" she added quite confidently.

Gasps filled the room. "Oh, good one!" Lindsay said, full of sarcasm, glaring back at Bailey. "Talk about original dialogue—like that's the first time I've heard *that* before!" She rolled her eyes big time at the chunky-butt across the table who had the nerve to talk to her this way.

Phillip, who was getting singed from the inferno raging inside Bailey, leaned over and whispered, "Honey, take a tip from Dionne Warwick and just *walk on by,*" he said, with a smooth sweep of his arm.

Bailey was tempted to continue to unload on the twit—who was rolling the ends of her hair around a finger, much the same way she had already managed to wrap Max around her finger—but she decided to take Phillip's advice and instead moved on to the next point on her agenda.

❧

At 3 o'clock, Peter entered Bailey's office after a late lunch, slumped into a chair at the writers' table, and lay down his head. "You look beat," Bailey said, as she pushed her portable TV back against the wall after viewing the day's episode. "Did you not sleep well last night?"

"I slept well, I just didn't get enough of it," he explained. "Alec wanted to play his favorite bedroom game last night—Crouching Tiger, Hidden Dragon." Peter grinned mischievously. "He's Siegfried...I'm Roy—*g-r-r-r!*"

Bailey could tell by his expression Peter was trying to sound ferocious, but the best he could produce was an effeminate trill of the tongue on the roof of his mouth. Even though Peter was a friend, they were still coworkers, and Peter sometimes ventured over the fine line between the two. She just hoped he didn't go into a blow-by-blow account.

"You don't look like you're having such a great day yourself," he responded.

"I can't stand it any more, Peter," she said, pacing irately. "That girl is the black hole of knowledge—she is sucking every educated thought right out of my head!" Bailey held her head to keep anything important from escaping. "I'm afraid I'm going to wake up one day as stupid as she is!" Her expression became grim. "And I think it might have already happened," she added, plopping into the chair beside him.

"What do you mean?"

"When I was getting ready for work this morning, I had the radio on, and I switched channels and caught the tail end of this song before they went to a commercial. And it was one of my favorite songs by Fleetwood Mac—one that I *know*—but the name just won't come to me, and it's driving me crazy!

"I can hear the whole song perfectly in my head…a pounding native drum beat that conjures up images of elephants lumbering down a dirt road in India, then their voices huff out this one word, it's the title of the song and I think of the whole album, but the only word that sounds right is 'Trunk!' and I know that's not right.

"It starts with a *T* and ends with a *K*—I remember those sounds distinctly, but goddamn it—I can't think of the friggin' word!"

"Maybe you should ask Lindsay," he said.

Bailey was surprised but encouraged. "What—you know Lindsey…Lindsey Buckingham—the guy who wrote the song?" she stammered.

"No, I meant Stubblefield."

Her face contorted. "Why would I ask her—she doesn't even know who the fuck *Elvis* is!"

"It was a joke. Jeez, have you lost your sense of humor too?"

"Oh, God! What if that's next?! I'll get brain lock

and won't be able to write and I'll lose my job and my condo and I'll end up a bag lady in Central Park." A second later she gasped. "Oh, my God—it's like the Stockholm syndrome. I'm starting to identify with this idiot in our midst!"

"Honey, you have got to stop this," Peter said seriously.

"I can't! She's pickling my brain, Peter! My brain won't work anymore. I'm seriously getting scared," she said, biting her nails absentmindedly. Then she had a flash of genius. "The Internet!" she cried, and rushed toward the computer on her desk.

"*No!*" Peter shouted, rising to his feet. "Don't do it!" he commanded. "Don't get on the Internet, don't call the radio station, don't ask anyone—you can do this yourself. Just program that computer in your head to search for the material requested and it'll come to you sooner or later. Don't let her win, Bailey," he said with encouragement. "Come on, now, you can do this."

Bailey went all limp and whiny. "But I'll be up all night trying to think of this on my own. I've already had seven hours to work on it, and I've got nothin'."

"So just program your brain to come up with it before midnight."

She let out a sigh and thought hard, going over the song in her head again. "Duh, duh, duh, *trunk*!" she puffed, with hands lurching out as if surprising someone. Then she shook her head angrily. "Wait, I've got it...Duh, duh, duh, *fuck*!" she shouted angrily before slumping into her chair.

"No, I don't think that's it either," Peter said, which

won him an icy glare, which in turn convinced him to stop poking the bear.

◈

Lindsay came floating in all dreamy-eyed 15 minutes late for the afternoon session that day, ignoring the business conversation going on at the table. "I don't understand why Beau isn't a movie star—he's so gorgeous," she sighed during a pause in the conversation.

Bailey tapped her fingers angrily on the round tabletop. "You mean *Mitch*," she said.

"I just don't understand why Hollywood hasn't scooped him up," Lindsay continued.

"You know, he is handsome enough to be in the movies," Rhonda said, causing Bailey great distress at having lost another of the brood to this ridiculous daydream.

"It's very simple." Bailey said sharply. "The average feature film takes 10 weeks to shoot. Soap contracts only allow actors six weeks off for other projects."

"I didn't know that," Max said, full of interest. "I mean, I knew actors had the six-week limit, but I didn't know why. How about that."

Bailey nodded. "Yeah, after the soaps lost Demi Moore and Kathleen Turner and a few others to the movies, they wised up and made it a standard clause. Why should they spend years and tons of money building these actors and their characters into audience-drawing entities, only to lose them to the movies? They got tired of being Hollywood's training ground."

"That's really why they changed their contracts?" Stephano asked.

"Yep," Bailey said, then laughed. "You should read the fine print of *our* contracts sometime," she said, shaking her head in pity.

"What do you mean?" Lindsay asked.

"Didn't you read the Kidney Clause?" she said, looking the girl in the eye.

Bailey had asked the question straight-faced, but the others grinned, realizing their head writer was just having some fun tormenting the neophyte.

"Well, the writers are kind of looked on as the ugly stepchildren kept hidden away upstairs in the attic, I'm sure you've noticed." Lindsay nodded to the affirmative, still locked onto Bailey's eyes. "The only time they bring us out is when one of the actors needs a kidney transplant or some other organ." Lindsay's mouth fell slightly open, not at all sure whether this tale of horror was fact or fiction. "Sure," Bailey said, pouring on the sincerity, "that's all we're good for around here: spare parts."

"Oh, my God," Lindsay whispered in shock.

Bailey smiled, feeling much better, and picked up where she had left off on the day's script.

❧

In the middle of Letterman's monologue that night, the phone rang at Peter's apartment. He was in bed still watching TV, Alec already sound asleep next to him. When he answered, there was only a one-word message from the other end:

"*Tusk!*"

"See," he said proudly, "I knew you could do it...now get some sleep."

The noise had roused Alec, who rolled over with squinty eyes full of sleep. "Who was that?" he groaned.

"It was just Bailey," Peter replied, having gone back to watching the show. "Go back to sleep, honey," Peter said, patting him on the shoulder.

"What did she say?"

"Tusk."

A long pause ensued while Alec waited for the information to compute, but it was too much for his sleep-filled brain. "O-o-o-kay," he said, and rolled back over.

Chapter Six

"I don't know if I'm ready for this," Bailey said.

"Sure you are," Peter replied enthusiastically. "You've had almost a month to get Miranda out of your system. Plus you've had nothing but aggravation at work lately from Clueless—you deserve to have some fun."

Peter had asked Bailey to join him and Alec for dinner at their home that weekend so he could reveal the name of the perfect woman he had selected for her. While Peter and Bailey cleared the table, Alec quietly adjourned to the living room so his partner could play matchmaker. "You sure you won't feel neglected in there all alone, sweetie?" Peter called out affectionately.

"No, I'm fine," Alec said, sitting in his chair, picking up the remote control.

Peter watched his lover, who was dressed in casual slacks, a comfortable cardigan sweater, and his favorite old loafers, as he settled into his chair and began flipping through the pages of the *TV Guide*. "My own Mr. Rogers," he cooed.

Bailey smiled. "No offense, but I've never understood how two people who are so different could be so compatible. He's so mild-mannered and you're...not. I can't believe you guys have been together eight years."

"Tell me. He's such a homebody. His idea of the perfect evening is dinner at home, a little TV, then a good romp in the sack before falling asleep."

Bailey laughed as she picked up the last of the silverware.

Peter leaned close to her ear. "And when I say 'a good romp,' I mean *a good romp*."

Her eyes widened. "Ahh, so that explains it."

"Honey, there is nothing like a great fuck to make two people compatible. Makes *all* the little habits and eccentricities tolerable."

Peter stood beside the empty table, his hands clasped in front of him, admiring his love, who was squinting hard, holding the guide very close to his face. "You know you need your glasses for reading," Peter scolded, but his comment went ignored. He shook his head hopelessly and turned to Bailey. "He's blind as a bat, but he refuses to wear his reading glasses in front of company. He's so vain."

"Why...are they really thick?" Bailey asked as she took a seat.

"Like two little Hubble Telescopes," Peter replied sadly.

From the living room, the two could hear Alec talking

to himself, reading off names of programs. "*Topless in Battle?* What the hell kind of war movie is that?" he said, sounding more angry than puzzled at the ridiculous title.

Peter rolled his eyes, stomped over to Alec, and jerked the guide out of his hands. "*Sleepless in Seattle!*" he announced, then slapped the guide back into Alec's hands and headed back to the dining room. "Put yer glasses on!" he shouted over his shoulder.

"*Sleepless in Seattle?*" Alec said with a snarl. "That's a chick flick."

Peter looked shocked. "Oh, and what do you want to watch—some war movie or one of those stupid *American Pie* 'hormonal boy trying to get some pussy' movies? You'd rather watch one of those dick flicks?"

Alec snorted in contempt and continued perusing the guide. "At least it's better than *Sleepless in Seattle*," he grumbled to himself.

Bailey cracked up but tried to control herself, not wanting to get caught up in this spat, should it escalate. Peter rolled his eyes as he sat next to Bailey then opened the buffet and took out several photo albums. "This, coming from a man who insists on chintz and chenille in the bedroom," he said.

A finger went to Bailey's temple and tapped while she seemed to recollect something. "Chintz and Chenille...didn't they have a hit song in the '70s?"

Peter and Bailey simultaneously broke into "Love Will Keep Us Together" and began dancing in their chairs, arms waving, fingers snapping to the beat, which caused Alec to give them a look and shake his head in pity.

"For a gay man, he has no fashion sense...*at o-o-o-w-w-l,*" Peter added in one of his frequent homages to Fran Drescher, *The Nanny* being his favorite TV show of all time.

After flipping through two of the albums and not finding the photo he was looking for, Peter pulled out a third and began a quick scan over the pages. Finally he stopped and pointed to a particular photo. "That's her," he said proudly. "She's *perfect* for you." He took the photo out and handed it to Bailey.

She checked out the picture of a tall, slender, raven-haired woman in jeans and a sweatshirt in a group photo taken at a Giants game. "Wow...she's gorgeous."

Peter took in a deep breath as though he smelled something delicious. "Honey, you'll cream your jeans when you see her in person. This picture does *not* do her justice...*does it, Alec?*" he shouted to his lover.

Alec didn't speak, but the big grin and raised eyebrows told Bailey he agreed with Peter's assessment.

Bailey figured if a gay man reacted that way about a woman, this chick must truly be hot. "Why is he grinning like that?" she whispered.

"Tell Bailey why you're grinning like a half-wit, honey!" Peter shouted as he perused more photos.

"Great tits!" Alec replied, cupping his hands at his chest.

In an attempt to explain to Bailey why Alec was lusting over a woman's breasts, Peter said in a pissy tone, "Cheyenne flashed him at a New Year's party once."

Bailey admired the picture a little longer. "Cheyenne, huh?" she said with a hint of a smile, liking the soft-sounding name as it floated from her lips.

"Cheyenne Cassidy," Peter said.

Bailey came out of her hormonal stupor for a moment and asked Peter about the woman's non-physical qualities. "Well, she graduated Yale Drama School and was an actress and chorus girl for about 10 years—did a lot of commercials and off-Broadway stuff, then a few years ago she started her own business." He couldn't remember exactly what her business was and asked Alec if he knew.

Alec, who was entranced by a rerun of *Three's Company,* said, "Some sort of cable talk show or something. Last I talked to her she said she'd just gone international...or syndicated—I'm not sure exactly."

"Anyway, she must be doing all right because she just moved into a Park Avenue apartment."

"O-o-o-h!" Bailey said, sounding impressed.

"O-o-o-h, indeed. She's smart, sexy, and successful...just like you, my dear," he said, patting Bailey on the hand. "You're perfect for each other," he added, sounding quite pleased with himself.

But Bailey remained hesitant. "If she's so great, how come she's available?"

Peter looked down his nose at her. "You're great, and you're available," he said. "So you two have a lot in common," he concluded. "You should get along great."

He watched Bailey as she considered things. "Shall I set it up for next Saturday night?" he said, coaxing her.

Bailey took in a deep breath and sighed. "What the hell," she said, handing him back the picture.

Peter smiled with great anticipation.

≥●

The reflection in the floor-length mirror in the dressing room at Bloomingdale's didn't tell her what she wanted to hear, so Bailey got dressed and pounded the pavement on Fifth Avenue for another hour until she found herself outside Bergdorf Goodman. She had been in there only once in her entire life as a teenager, and it had proved to be such a horrendous experience that she'd vowed never to attempt it again.

There was nothing in life Bailey hated more than shopping. The reason was because it only reminded her of her physical shortcomings. She was 5-foot-8 and 162 pounds of muscle...well, mostly muscle. On a cab ride a few weeks ago she noticed her stomach jiggling under her shirt whenever they hit a bump, which had to be some middle-age curse that was now upon her.

She had never had a waistline, and her wide pelvic bones gave her a smokestack torso. And of course, a wide pelvis meant a wide backside too. Thus, having been blessed with a big butt, no waist, and no boobs, it was hell trying to find clothes in the women's section that fit properly. But she simply couldn't go out on her first date tonight with a beautiful Park Avenue babe wearing Levi's, so Bailey reluctantly went inside.

To the left of the entrance was a huge marquee with a floor-by-floor listing of each designer. They were all there: Oscar de la Renta, Michael Kors, Versace,

Carolina Herrera, Narciso Rodriguez, Buccellati, Gaultier, Gianfranco Ferre, and dozens more she had never heard of. Her head was spinning. There was even a restaurant of the fifth floor with the very chic name Cafe on 5ive. Great. Now she could spend the entire day shopping and be one of the "ladies who lunch," just like Patsy and Edina. Yeah, right.

No sooner had she started her journey than her bubble was burst, for Bailey was dressed in old jeans, a bulky cotton ramie sweater with a colorful geometric print, and black boots, which did not meet the dress code for shopping at Bergdorf's or qualify her for any courtesy from the salesgirls. Apparently one had to be decked out in designer duds plus have on $100,000 worth of jewelry to get any respect or service around there. Yep, this was just the way she remembered it.

At first she didn't mind being left alone to shop around, but when she couldn't find the Victor Costa section, which was listed on the marquee as being on the sixth floor, she asked a passing salesgirl—totally decked out—who didn't seem to be with a customer, as she had no clothing draped over her arm like most of the others. At least Bailey *tried* to ask, because the salesgirl completely ignored her when she said, "Excuse me, can you tell me where the Victor Costa section is?" and just kept right on walking, doing that weird supermodel walk, like she was in dire need of a hip replacement.

Bailey couldn't believe her rudeness, so she decided to dish it back and shouted after the woman. "Hey— I'm talking to you!" she growled.

The salesgirl stopped, put a hand on her hip, and did a swivel-turn. With a look of complete disgust, she gave the customer a "tsk," let out a heavy sigh, and said, "We don't *carry* Victor Costa," as though Bailey were the biggest moron in the universe.

Without even waiting for a reply, the salesgirl turned and started walking away again. Bailey was boiling by that point and stomped after her. She grabbed the girl by the elbow, jerked her around, and said, "Hey, honey, don't talk to me like I'm some kind of idiot—Victor Costa is listed downstairs on your marquee, for your information!"

Miss Hoity Toity pulled her arm away, looking concerned that she may have contracted fleas from this bag lady who had the nerve to touch her, and huffed, "We haven't carried Victor Costa for ages."

Bailey gave her back that pissy little "tsk" and said, "Well, why don't you take it off the damn marquee then? And where do you get off giving me this attitude for asking a legitimate question?"

She gave Bailey the jazz hands and eye roll. "I don't have time to waste on you," she said, and walked away again.

Of course, Bailey followed after her like a rabid Chihuahua nipping at the girl's Bruno Maglis. "Look, sister, just because I'm wearing jeans doesn't mean I don't have money. For your information, I have $100,000 in my checking account that I'm planning on spending today."

The salesgirl gave that slow turn again—while Bailey rubbed her nose to make sure it wasn't growing—and with a smirk the girl said, "I'm *not* impressed. Our average customer spends half a million dollars a year."

Hands on her hips, Bailey glared back at the horrid creature. "And you think that gives *you* the right to cop this high-and-mighty attitude, because *other* people spend a lot of money in this store? That's a pretty big leap for someone who's *just* a salesgirl," and *she* turned around and walked off. What—a—bitch!

Bailey consoled herself in the Versace section, modeling a black crepe de chine pantsuit in the triple mirror, torquing and twisting to see how the pants looked from behind. A different salesgirl was in the next dressing room collecting unwanted garments from another customer, so Bailey asked for her opinion. "Tell me the truth...do these make my butt look big?" she asked.

The girl gave her a mere glance before saying, "No, dear, your butt looks big all on its own."

Gee, thanks so much. "I guess I'll try these instead," she said, grabbing another pair of pants from a hanger.

"I think those are a little too small for you," the salesgirl said, as though it should be obvious to anyone.

"But don't they have some spandex in them?" Bailey said, holding the pants up to her hips.

The girl raised an eyebrow. "Yes, but they're still governed by the laws of physics."

Bailey stood there reeling for a second, then dropped the pants on the floor right at the bitch's feet and slammed the dressing room door in her face. Yep, this was *definitely* the way she remembered it.

Bailey finally found a gorgeous charcoal-gray,

wool-blend Armani pantsuit that miraculously fit as though it had been custom tailored for her. She admired herself in the triple mirror. It was stunning. And if it had a decent price on it, she'd take it. She felt the price tag up her left sleeve and pulled it out to see. Yeeoow! The price was equally stunning: $4,000...marked down from $6,000. No doubt this garment was part of the big Year End Sale. But somehow 33% off didn't seem like such a bargain with that many zeroes involved.

After she picked her eyeballs up off the floor and put them back in their sockets, she started unbuttoning the jacket. Then it dawned on her that the price tag had been concealed up the sleeve, which meant she could look like 4,000 bucks on her date and make a great first impression, then pull the return scheme and bring it back Monday morning for a full refund. Genius! And losing a big commission would serve these bitches right for being so mean to her. She buttoned the jacket again and turned side to side. This was the most gorgeous suit she had ever seen, and she was going to enjoy it to the max for the next 72 hours.

She took the suit to one of the cashiers, an older yet impeccably dressed woman who complimented Bailey on her good taste as she rang up a decent commission for having done not a damn thing. Bailey leaned over the counter toward this kinder, gentler saleswoman and asked, "Excuse me, but what would you say the average customer spends here during a year?"

The lady carefully put the suit in a garment bag

and tied the bottom in a knot. "Our sales statistics that just came out say our average customer last year spent $487,000."

All Bailey could do was shake her head in bewilderment. That was slightly more than her annual salary before taxes. What kind of people have that kind of money to spend on clothes every year? It was beyond her.

Chapter Seven

Bailey called for her date at 8 sharp that evening. The uniformed doorman asked her to be seated on one of the two tufted leather sofas in the lobby while he rang Ms. Cassidy's apartment. She carefully sat down, not wanting to crease her new pants or jacket, and nervously checked that the price tag shoved up her sleeve wasn't showing. Soon Bailey heard the ping of the elevator and footsteps coming toward her.

She thought she'd died and gone to heaven. Cheyenne looked like a model in one of those shampoo commercials and seemed to be walking in slow motion, accentuating every movement as she stepped. She was 5-foot-11 in flats, wearing a long, black clingy dress that accented her slender curves. It was slit high on the left thigh, and the spaghetti straps showed off the great muscle tone in her arms. She had dark, smoldering, wicked eyes; full, pouting red lips; and jet-black hair resting on her shoulders that bounced sensually as she walked...as did her gorgeous breasts.

My, oh, my, Peter had been telling the truth. This girl did have a great set of firm C-cups on her. Standing up all on their own too, with no bra underneath pushing them up—Bailey could tell by the way her erect nipples were about to rip through the delicate fabric covering them. At that moment, she felt like the luckiest lesbian on earth. This was the kind of woman she'd dreamed about all her life. It made her afternoon at Hell on 5ive worth every insult.

A crisp chill filled the air, and they both felt like walking the six blocks to Le Bordeaux. Manhattan seemed beautiful to Bailey, with a clear sky above and the unusually clean sidewalks one always found on Park Avenue. All the men they passed on the street turned and ogled Cheyenne as she bounced past, which created in Bailey the turmoil of flattery over her own good taste in women colliding with her jealousy.

Once at the restaurant, the internal conflict continued when their waiter, who was obviously flirting with Cheyenne, brought them a platter of crab-stuffed mushroom caps—on the house. Bailey watched her date smile playfully at the young man as she bit into one of the delicacies in a rather teasing fashion, which caused the young man to blush and scamper away. Then Cheyenne either noticed something in Bailey's expression or felt something in the air that prompted her to say, "Oh, please, this is nothing. Men have always flirted with me like this," she said, licking her fingertips. "When I was in high school, they'd buy me stuffed animals and chocolates. When I got older, they started buying me jewelry, clothes, cars, all with the hope that I'd sleep with them. Men are such idiots," she concluded, wiping a little oil from her mouth with her napkin. "Although it did come in handy now and then," she added matter-of-factly.

Bailey liked the way Cheyenne referred to this power of hers as "It," as though "It" were an entity one could acquire and possess and control; as though "It" were a secret weapon she used to turn men's spines to jelly.

Cheyenne proceeded to tell Bailey about the time during her senior year in high school when she had been driving to Yale for a frat party and had an open bottle of vodka in the car. "I was speeding and got pulled over by the highway patrol," she said, giggling. "These two beefy patrolmen took a look at my legs when I got out of my car, and they went apoplectic." Bailey had no doubt that was right.

"So there I was—speeding, a minor in possession of alcohol, and driving with an open bottle in the car," she said, counting the infractions on her fingers. "I had to think fast, so I told them my mother would be worried because I'd gotten a late start out of town and she might think I had been in a wreck, so I was just trying to get there fast so I could call Mommy. And they let me off with a warning!" she said with a cruel laugh that seemed to be more for the two patrolmen than about the situation in general. Then Cheyenne's dark eyes glittered with power and confidence. "You think they would have let a *guy* off like that?" she asked, then threw back her raven tresses with a "Ha!"

Bailey knew she was right. Hell, a less attractive female wouldn't have had that kind of luck.

"Jesus, I can't tell you how many times I've been stopped for ridiculous things, like my taillight supposedly being out or my turn light blinking, but of course when I'd get out and check, everything was suddenly fine. Then they'd ask me to have coffee after they got off their shift. No, thanks. Then—oh, this is the best! The time I went parking with this guy and had just given him a blow job."

Bailey's eyes got wide, then she looked left and right to be sure no one had heard her. Cheyenne apparently had no qualms about discussing fellatio in a public place.

"Anyway, he was still reeling from this orgasmic stupor I'd put him in, and he hit the car next to us when he changed lanes without looking." She read the puzzled look on Bailey's face and shrugged it off. "Come on, I was in college—it was during one of my experimental phases."

Bailey nodded understandingly, then rested her chin in her palm, anxious to hear the rest of this story.

"Anyway, he didn't have insurance, so he hopped the curb and started driving that Mercedes convertible of his through the park like it was a Hummer, with this guy he'd just run into hot on our trail. We finally ditched him, and he told me to get out in case he got caught 'cause he didn't want me going to jail with him. So I ran through the park to the street and came upon a cop who was parked doing his paperwork after giving someone a ticket.

"Well, I always cry when I run long distances—my lungs start hurting and I can't breathe—so I started crying when I got up to this cop car, and I boo-hooed my words out, asking him if he would take me home. On the way home, he asked what happened, and I said I had been with a bunch of friends and they started acting weird, and the guy driving was getting really reckless and I was scared he was going to kill us in a wreck."

Something suddenly occurred to Bailey—how easily it seemed to be for Cheyenne to lie and make up such detailed stories on the spur of the moment, as if she'd been honing that skill her whole life.

"So he looked right in my eyes and said, 'That's not really what happened, now, is it?' Well, I just knew I was busted, so I started to confess, and I said, 'No, I got out of the car because the person driving—' and he finished my sentence by saying, '—was doing drugs, right?' Well, a light bulb went on over my head, and I blubbered, 'Y-e-e-e-s!' then turned on the waterworks." She doubled over from laughing so hard.

"So what happened then?"

"Oh, he took me home but didn't come in to say anything to my parents, because I'd been a good girl and gotten out of that car and not let my evil drug-doing friends influence me." Her eyes rolled. "He didn't want to get a sweet, innocent girl like me in trouble just for hanging out with a bad element." Her smile suddenly turned to a smirk. "I swear, men are such horny fuckers. They go goofy at the sight of a pretty girl, especially one with a great rack."

At that moment Bailey understood what "It" was. Cheyenne was gorgeous and sexy...and she *knew* it. And that was a lethal combination for any woman to possess. Bailey knew right then that a relationship with this woman would be double trouble, because she'd not only have to worry about other girls flirting with her partner, but guys too—and that was way more competition than she was used to dealing with.

Cheyenne was still going on about what fools men were, with Bailey hanging on every word that came out of those luscious lips, when she suddenly stopped in mid-sentence and frowned. "What's that?" Cheyenne said.

Suddenly Bailey saw a hand coming right toward her face, and instinctively she jerked it away from its palm pedestal. A rush of insecurity swept through her. Oh, God—what was it? A spice from lunch caught between her front teeth? Crust in the corner of her eye? What god-awful thing was Cheyenne reaching out to correct?

"Oh," Cheyenne said with a chortle as she touched the sleeve of Bailey's jacket, "you forgot to take the price tag off your suit," and in an instant she had ripped the white cardboard off the skinny plastic tab. Bailey's eyes got as big as saucers. *N-o-o-o!*

Her heart rate doubled, and she gasped so hard it almost extinguished the candle on their table. Automatically her trembling hands reached out toward the little white piece of cardboard in her date's hands.

Cheyenne's eyes popped too, after she read the tag. "Wow! $4,000!" She looked the big woman up and down. "I'm impressed," she said as she ripped up the tag and sprinkled the tiny white pieces onto her bread plate.

Bailey was barely able to hold back the tears, and in her head she heard herself yelling at Cheyenne: $4,000 is right, honey—for one damn suit! You *better* be impressed 'cause that's $4,000 I'll never get back!

Dozens of worthwhile things Bailey could have spent that money on bombarded her brain. A wave of nausea swept over her, and she rubbed her throbbing temples. Oh, well...there went her vacation to St. Croix this summer. She let out a sigh and forced a pitiful smile. No use crying over spilt milk. "Thanks" was all the response she could muster.

The writer couldn't say whether her meal had been any good, because the deep blue funk she was in over that damn suit had caused the part of her brain connected to her taste buds to black out. After paying the check, which Bailey had just enough cash to cover, the couple stood to leave. "Wait a second," Cheyenne said, taking Bailey by the shoulder, "turn around. I think there's something on the back of your pants."

Great. Bailey immediately thought of those old vaudeville routines where someone pulls a loose string and the next thing you know, that person is completely unraveled and standing naked onstage in front of a bunch of strangers. Then she figured she had probably sat in gum and would end up with a hole the size of a gumball in the seat of her pants and never be able to wear the damn thing again, now that it was hers.

Cheyenne took a good look at Bailey's backside,

then a wicked grin spread across her face. "Nope, lookin' good," she said, then gave Bailey's right cheek a firm, lingering squeeze that made the big woman do a little jig. Bailey turned bright red when she saw all the people around them who had caught the act, and she quickly guided Cheyenne to the exit.

꧁꧂

Cheyenne's 10th-floor apartment was an art deco dream, full of high-priced antiques, and Bailey was getting the grand tour, which she took as a good sign. The three-bedroom apartment had more than twice as much square footage as Bailey's, with a master bathroom the size of the writer's living room. A black marble Jacuzzi tub in the center of the room was big enough to swim in. "It's great for those cold winter nights," Cheyenne said, "and for when I'm in-between girlfriends," she added with a naughty tone.

Suddenly a picture flashed inside Bailey's head of Cheyenne totally naked, legs spread in a big V in front of one of the Jacuzzi jets, throwing her head back and screaming in ecstasy as she was overcome by a powerful orgasm. Then she noticed an intense tingling between her own legs.

Cheyenne showed off all her prized possessions, which were obviously expensive and well-crafted, but something about this style seemed cold to Bailey—all the sharp edges, the geometric lines, the shiny polished brass and chrome. She fingered the leaded glass shade of a lamp on the table beside the living room couch, admiring its intricate pattern. "I almost bought a Tiffany reproduction very similar to this one that I saw at an estate sale last year."

"It's not a reproduction," Cheyenne purred.

Bailey quickly withdrew her hand and put both hands safely in her pockets. She had just spent $4,000 on a suit—she didn't need to spend $200,000 replacing a *real* Tiffany lamp.

She admired a beautiful rosewood table with a goatskin top in front of the couch, then commented on the strange-looking table against the wall a few feet behind the couch. "It's a gueridon with a sharkskin top," Cheyenne said. "It was designed by J. Leleu," she said, adding that he had been a French designer in the 1940s. She continued pointing at various pieces in the room. "This is by Rene Prou...this is by Raymond Subes."

The names meant nothing to Bailey, but she guessed they had been top art deco designers in their day. "Sounds like the French were really into art deco," she said, not knowing what else to say.

"They were," Cheyenne replied. "And speaking of sounds, would you like some music?"

Bailey felt that was a bit of a stretch for a segue but decided to let it slide, saying, "Sure."

Cheyenne flipped through a tall rack of CDs then pulled one out. "How about some Queen?"

"Works for me," Bailey said with a shrug.

The tall woman slinked over to the stereo system and set the disc on the player. "I love this album."

"Which one is it?"

"*Jazz.*"

"Yep," Bailey said, bobbing her head, "that was a good one."

The song "Bicycle Race" began and Cheyenne sighed with fond memories. "God, all these songs take me back to my high school days. At every party I went to there was always a Queen song in the mix." She turned to Bailey. "This song reminds me of the first time I ever kissed a boy. It was at a party after my debutante ball."

This announcement took Bailey by surprise. "You were a deb?"

"I was a Long Island debutante a few Novembers back," she confessed, as though she couldn't believe she had ever done anything so ridiculous.

"November? I thought I always saw pictures from the debutante balls in the paper around May and June?"

"No, the season is traditionally November through January—why, I don't know, because it's freezing cold and not compatible with strapless gowns, which is what everyone who had even the slightest bustline wanted to wear."

She slipped deeper into the memory. "The debutante ball," she said wistfully, yet with a hint of sarcasm, "the time when a young girl of marriageable age is welcomed into the world of civic responsibility and social awareness." Her smile turned sour. "What a bunch of crap," she blurted out, then went over to the bar and began pouring two glasses of bourbon without even asking Bailey what she'd like.

"And what a barbaric ceremony," she added. "I felt like a virgin being sacrificed at the altar of a bunch of horny Long Island boys." Cheyenne cupped her hands like a megaphone at her mouth. "Here she is, boys! She's ready to be impregnated to breed another generation of rich spoiled bastards—*c-o-o-o-me a-a-a-nd get it*!" She hollered like a cowpoke on a cattle drive calling the other wranglers to the chuck wagon. Then she smiled again. "Boy, did *they* get a surprise."

Bailey, herself, was surprised. "You mean you came out in the '70s? Wow, that was pretty bold. Weren't you afraid of being ostracized?"

"Actually, that was what I was hoping for—to get out of that superficial world of money and booze, and philandering husbands and dutiful wives who put up a brave front for society. It's so sickening...so fake." She joined Bailey on the couch and handed her a bourbon on the rocks.

"Did your family accept it?" Bailey said, politely sipping at the drink, even though she didn't like bourbon.

Cheyenne let out a chortle. "They accepted it the same way they accepted every other crisis they had to deal with...by ignoring it. They pretended it didn't exist. Then over the years, they pretended *I* didn't exist," she said coldly.

Suddenly Cheyenne felt the unmistakable pall she had cast over this date and quickly changed the subject. "That's a nice suit," she said in a teasing tone. "Did you go out and buy that just for me?" She grinned so big it made Bailey blush.

"I did," the stocky woman readily confessed as she

stood up and walked about in an effort to let the blood that had rushed to her cheeks get back into circulation. "And let me tell you, I went through hell to get it."

She then related the story of her shopping fiasco at Bergdorf's and her displeasure with the size of her rear end. "It's too big," she stated plainly, thrusting her hands onto her hips, a gesture more of disgust than to illustrate her point.

Cheyenne slinked up to the woman, slid her arms through Bailey's arms, around her back, and down to her derriere, hugging her tight. "Yeah, but it's a *great* ass," she said, just before laying one on Bailey.

When their kiss broke, Cheyenne's lips whispered into Bailey's ear as they nibbled on it. "I've been dying to get my hands on those gorgeous cheeks all night long," she panted. "I *love* big-assed women!" She kissed Bailey again—this time it was a long, wet kiss, all the while her hands roving over every inch of Bailey's broad butt. "I don't mean the Jennifer Lopez kind— the bubble butt that bounces and jiggles all over the place. I mean the broad-boned hips with tight buns like yours."

She grabbed each cheek firmly, then pushed their pelvises together and held on tight. "Something about that gorgeous curve from behind gets me s-o-o-o wet!" she growled as she took one of Bailey's hands and slid it underneath the slit in her dress, then between her legs. Bailey was shocked for two reasons: First, because Cheyenne wasn't wearing any panties; second, because she was, indeed, wet as a Slip N' Slide. A hot flush came over Bailey again, setting her face on fire. She was so pent-up after almost three months without sex that her hormones were about to bust through the dam. So she returned the big, wet kiss.

Cheyenne took her tongue and flicked an ear lobe, making the recipient groan with delight. "Aah, does Bailey need a good tongue lashing?" she said wickedly just before running her tongue temptingly over her own full, red lips.

Bailey couldn't believe this was happening to her. A gorgeous, sexy woman wanted *her*. But sex on a first date? Oh, hell—so what if she had some meaningless healthy sex with someone she didn't care about and barely knew? Other people jumped into the sack on a first date all the time. For once, she was entitled. And it wasn't like Cheyenne was unwilling—God *knows* the girl was willing. She glanced down at the fine cleavage and breasts pressed against her own. What the fuck. "Let's go," she said.

Red lips parted into a tantalizing smile, and the woman in black led Bailey into the bedroom and, piece by piece, stripped her naked. She playfully pushed Bailey onto the large brass bed, and Bailey eagerly scooted to the center where she lay, arms outstretched toward Cheyenne, waiting for her seductress to join her. Instead, Cheyenne slithered over to her walk-in closet and disappeared momentarily. Bailey's creative mind ran rampant wondering what the hell this woman was going to fetch, but when Cheyenne returned, she was carrying only a Bloomie's Big Brown Bag filled with different colored feather boas. Bailey exhaled a sigh of relief. Is that all? So she was going to get the

Dance of the Seven Boas. Perfectly harmless.

Cheyenne unzipped her dress and let it plummet to the floor, leaving her buck naked. She wrapped the black boa around her neck, letting the tail ends fall down over her voluptuous breasts, much to Bailey's disappointment since it obscured the gorgeous mounds of flesh from her sight. Then she wrapped another boa around her right arm, one around her left, and one around each thigh.

Cheyenne climbed aboard Bailey, sitting atop her pelvic area, and took the white boa from around her right arm and tickled Bailey's left nipple until it became erect. Then she intertwined her fingers with Bailey's left hand and leaned forward for what Bailey expected to be a juicy kiss. To her surprise, Cheyenne stretched their arms out full-length and started tying Bailey's wrist to the brass headboard with the boa. Ah, so that's what this chick was into.

Next, the red boa was removed from around her other arm and she tied up Bailey's right arm. She did the same with the two boas from around her thighs, tying Bailey's ankles to the bed. And then she began sliding off the black boa from around her neck.

Since there were no more limbs to attach to the bed, Bailey couldn't imagine what she was going to tie up with this last string of feathers. Cheyenne crawled back onto the bed between Bailey's legs and began gently dragging the feathers between the stocky legs. First she teased Bailey's muff, then she drew the fluffy feathers right down the center of her body, tickling her with feather after feather after feather. She continued this treatment until her victim groaned loudly. "I think you're ready," the vixen growled hungrily.

"What now, my love?" Bailey teased.

Cheyenne jumped off the bed and stood spread eagle in all her naked glory. "It's showtime!" she shouted, then scurried off into the closet again.

Moments later, she came out dressed in a skin-licking black rubber catsuit with her voluminous breasts barely squeezed in behind the zipper.

"Let me guess, are you supposed to be Catwoman?" Bailey asked.

"No, I'm Mona," she said with a strange grin.

It took only a second for Bailey to notice there was indeed something different in her eyes, something wicked, nasty, and dangerous. "Mona?" she said, looking at the woman in shiny black. "Great," she mumbled as she rolled her eyes, "Peter's fixed me up with Sybil."

Mona turned and laughed, flashing dark eyes. "Honey, there's a Sybil in all of us—it's just a matter of letting the right girl out at the right time," she said with an innocent shrug.

Then she wheeled out a small antique tea table with a tiny round Internet camera and a selection of sexual Tinker Toys that made Bailey's eyes come out of their sockets. "What the hell are you doing?" she said with some urgency, trying to control her panic.

The woman looked genuinely puzzled. "I thought Peter told you. I have an Internet sex show—Mona's Midnight Sexcapades. I perform live sex acts with a weekly guest for $39.95 an hour. And I'm making a *fortune* from it!" she added with great glee. Bailey's head fell back and her mind went reeling. "Men are such perverts," Cheyenne grumbled as she connected the wires from the camera to the back of her computer.

Bailey turned her face as far away from the camera as possible. "Please tell me that thing's not on!" she shouted.

"Not yet. Not for another..." she checked the clock on her bedside table, "four and a half minutes. The show always begins at the stroke of midnight," she said, setting an automatic timer on the camera.

Holy shit! Now Bailey panicked. *Her* face and nude body—including her big ass—broadcast all over the world into homes of people she would never meet? The thought was just too damn creepy. She wrestled mightily with the boa constrictions, but to no avail. She expected them to come apart at the first yank and feathers to go flying, but these things must have been bound with some space-age polymer—whatever it was, it was digging into her skin and it hurt. "Uh, could we not do this tonight?" she suggested, just wanting to cover up.

Mona's arms dropped to her side and she stood, pouting. "But you said you wanted to have sex with me."

"I do, just not with the whole world watching!"

The woman in black sat down on the bed beside Bailey and caressed her face. "Aw, feeling a little shy this first time?"

A laugh popped out. "Honey, *shy* doesn't even come close!" she said, fidgeting hopelessly.

Mona folded her arms. "I see," she said flatly. All the playfulness and passion had disappeared and she was strictly business. "Well, sorry, sugartush...no camera, no sex."

While Bailey wrestled with the tough decision, Mona began rubbing her hands up the curves of her own hips, then around and around on her firm breasts, squeezing and pushing them together as she writhed in an erotic motion, back and forth to the music in the background, with expressions of extreme ecstasy. She climbed onto the bed and began doing the same thing to Bailey's body, touching, teasing, tickling. Suddenly Bailey flinched, which caused Mona to stop. "But I thought you enjoyed it when I touched you like this," she said with pouty lips just before she leaned over and sucked gently on Bailey's nipple, "and this," she said before sucking on the other nipple.

This sent Bailey's conscience into a battle with her desires. She kept up her resistance fairly well until Cheyenne moved down and began using her highly talented tongue. Chills of lust shot through the big woman's belly, up to her nipples, then through her arms and legs. "Oh, God," Bailey groaned. When she caught her breath, she looked the woman in the eye. "Could you...just...put that pillowcase over my face?"

Mona's eyes beamed with delight as she licked her lips. "O-o-o-h—kinky!" But then she jumped off the bed and headed back to the closet, which scared the hell out of Bailey. "I have this executioner's hood instead?" she said as an inquiry, dangling the black hood in her raised hand.

Bailey took a split second to think about it, then said eagerly, "Works for me!"

Cheyenne gently pulled the mask over Bailey's head, making sure the holes were in their proper places. Then she grabbed the stereo remote and pushed the select button with glee. In the seconds while the song she had chosen was cuing up on the CD, Cheyenne turned dramatically to the camera just before the *click*.

"Welcome to Mona's Midnight Sexcapades!" she shouted as "Fat Bottomed Girls" came ringing in from the stereo. Mona looked at Bailey like she was a box of Godiva chocolates. "My favorite song," she purred, then began pleasuring Bailey in the most bizarre, yet thorough ways.

&

At 10 minutes after 3, Peter and Alec were awakened by the phone ringing on the bedside table. Peter answered. "Come get me," Bailey groaned weakly.

"Bailey?" he said, half-asleep. "Where are you?"

"Cheyenne's."

"What's the matter?"

She hesitated a moment. "I can't walk and I don't have the cash for a cab."

This shook the sleep out of Peter's brain. "You can't walk?! Oh, my God—what happened? Did you fall? Are you hurt?"

"Just hurry," she moaned.

&

Peter's BMW pulled up to the curb outside Cheyenne's apartment, and Bailey, who had been sitting on the stoop, came walking over like Roy Rogers after being in the saddle on a month-long cattle drive. Peter's mouth dropped.

"What in the world happened to you, girl?" he asked as Bailey gingerly sat down and closed the car door.

"It's...nothing," she groaned.

He took a moment and looked her over for signs of cuts or bruises. "Well, did you fall down? Is anything broken?"

"I wouldn't be at all surprised," she mumbled. "I'll be fine, really." She squirmed, trying to get comfortable as they drove through the empty New York streets.

Several blocks later Bailey groused, "I thought you said Cheyenne had a talk show?"

"She does. At least I'm pretty sure that's what she does."

"Not quite, Sherlock...it's a live Internet sex show."

His eyes inflated like balloons. "Oh, my God!" he exclaimed with a laugh.

"Mona's Midnight Sexcapades," she announced.

Peter laughed even harder. "You're kidding! Well, it's a good thing you found out early in the game. Ah!" he said, putting a hand to his heart, "I had no idea!"

After a long silence, a suspicion crept into his brain. He turned to Bailey. "You didn't?!"

No response.

His eyes widened. "You *did?*"

Again, no response.

His jaw dropped to the floorboard as his head

darted side to side from the shock, causing Bailey to fear they might run off the road. "You were tonight's main attraction on Mona's Midnight Sexcapades?" he shouted incredulously. Then he suddenly pretended to be honored. "Oh, my God!" he gushed with awe. "I'm sitting in the car with an international porn queen!"

"Knock it off," Bailey growled, pulling on the inseam of her pants to loosen things up down there.

Peter bounced in his seat with mock excitement. "Can I have your autograph?"

"Cut it out!" she said a little more forcefully.

They drove along in silence, but only for a few minutes. "What on earth did she do to you?"

Bailey took in a deep breath and rolled her eyes. "You know that weird-looking kitchen utensil with the funny little—"

"*Stop!*" he shouted, holding up his right hand to block the words as he gave her the back of his head. "I do *not* want to hear any more."

Halfway home Peter asked, "How in the world did she wrangle you into this?"

"With surprisingly little effort," Bailey said, amazed at her willingness to have sex with a total stranger...on the Internet! She buried her face in her hands. "God, I'm so pathetic."

"Dear Bailey," Peter said, shaking his head, "dear, sweet, horny Bailey."

"I was! I was *so horny,*" she whined, practically pleading for forgiveness from the gods. "I hadn't had sex in *three months*! A major hormonal build-up will make you do crazy things sometimes. I just went temporarily insane!"

"Three months? I can't even imagine." Peter waited a few moments, then raised an eyebrow. "Was it good?" he asked, dying to hear the dish.

Bailey stared off into space. "She kept me teetering on the brink for over *two hours*! Somehow she knew just when my body was on the edge, and she'd stop— over, and over, and over...my God, when I finally came, I *know* I shattered windows in half that building. I swear to God, Peter," she said, looking him in the eye, "it was the most intense orgasm I have ever had...aah!" She groaned as she grasped the lapels of her new jacket and held them to her breasts, closing her eyes in fond remembrance.

"S-o-o-o...are you going to see her again?"

She looked at him like he was crazy to even ask. "I don't think so," Bailey said. "She's a great fuck, but she's just a little too kinky for me. But thanks for trying."

As he turned on to Bailey's street, he felt compelled to give his friend some advice. "You know the old saying...if at first you don't succeed, try, try again."

Bailey sat up, then grimaced from the pain. "No! Please! Do *not* fix me up with any more blind dates. It's gonna take me a while to heal from this one. Thanks, but no thanks."

Her words had no effect, and Peter smiled with superiority. "I'll give you a few weeks to get over this, then I'll fix you up with Ms. Right—you wait and see," he said with a wink.

Bailey didn't have the strength to argue with Dolly Levi over in the driver's seat, so she closed her eyes again. Then something dawned on her that made her brown eyes snap open. "I just paid *$4,000* for one fuck," she muttered in amazement.

Peter frowned, pondering this announcement. "Well...that doesn't sound right. Hell, Richard Gere only paid $3,000 for an entire week with Julia Roberts."

Bailey just closed her eyes again and started worrying about how she was going to make it up all those steps in the front of her building.

Chapter Eight

"Uh-oh...what's wrong?" Max asked. He knew just by looking at what Bailey had brought for lunch that her life was out of whack, because whenever things went wrong Bailey ate weird stuff. Today it was the Big Daddy of them all: Toasted onion bagel with cream cheese, bacon, avocado, tomato and black olives with the usual Welch's concord grape juice—the two *always* had to go together. Today Bailey craved the potent combo as the result of her disastrous date with Cheyenne over the weekend.

"If I didn't know you as well as I do, I'd think you were pregnant," Max added, grimacing at her bagel.

Lindsay immediately perked up and stared directly at Bailey's abdominal area. "She can't have kids?" the blond said. "Oh, how sad," she lamented, taking a bite of her sandwich. "You know, one of my best friends found out she was barren—and this was only a year after she'd gotten married. That is so sad."

A hush fell over the room. Everyone else on the staff knew Bailey was a lesbian, but they never discussed her sex life at the office.

"She's not barren," Max said in a clinical, subdued tone.

Lindsay looked at him with a wrinkled brow. "Did she have a bicycle accident as a kid or something?"

Everyone watched Max's words go right over the empty head. Bailey wanted to chime in but had a mouthful of bagel sandwich. Max rolled his eyes. "No, she didn't fall off a bike," was his lame response.

The girl's head cocked like a dog hearing its master's voice coming out of an answering machine. "Then why is it out of the question for her to be pregnant?"

Bailey finally swallowed and her hands went up. "Hello! I'm right here!" she shouted, then wiped her mouth with a napkin. "And can we stay out of my uterus, please?! Jesus—I feel like my feet are up in the stirrups and I'm scooching to the edge of the table."

That put the others momentarily off their food, but this scene was too good to pass up, so they all stayed put.

Lindsay looked at Bailey, then went straight to the source. "So why can't you be pregnant?"

Everyone waited anxiously for the response. Bailey's eyes locked onto Lindsay's. "Because I don't date men," she said slowly and matter-of-factly.

Lindsay frowned again. "Then, that would make you..."

Bailey exaggeratedly smiled and said, "Come on, come on—you can say it."

"A lesbian?" Lindsay said timidly.

Bailey clapped her hands in joy. "I *knew* you could say it!" she shouted with mock delight. "And your tongue didn't fall out or anything!"

Lindsay pouted at being made fun of. "I'm sorry, it's just that I've never met a lesbian before."

Mouths fell open around the table. "Now wait a minute," Phillip said, "you went to college at one of the Seven Sisters, and you don't think a-one of them sisters was a lesbian?" He laughed fiercely. "I'm bettin' you know *plenty* of lesbians."

Lindsay's eyes grew wide with shock and a hint of panic. "Absolutely not! They—they would have told me."

Bailey snickered. "Yeah, that's the first thing we say when we meet someone. 'Hi! I'm Tiffany...and I'm a lesbian!'" she said in a high-pitched, feminine voice.

"Well, how else would they get the word out to attract other lesbians?"

"Oh, we have our codes," Bailey replied mysteriously, "subtle ways of letting one another know we're a member of the club." Everyone recognized that familiar glint in Bailey's eyes—the one that glowed when her wit was turned on high.

This response piqued Lindsay's curiosity. "Like what?"

Bailey leaned in close to the girl and looked her in the eye. "You know how sometimes songs aren't really about what you think they're about, like 'Puff the Magic Dragon'? Some people think it's a fairy tale about a dragon, but most people think it's about smoking marijuana?"

"Yeah?" Lindsay looked suspicious; the others simply

wondered where in the world Bailey was going with this.

"Well, remember the television show *Laverne & Shirley?*"

The others got it right away, but Miss Thick-As-A-Brick didn't have a clue. "Uh-huh?" she said.

"Do you remember what Laverne used to wear on the left side of all her shirts and sweaters?"

They all knew the exact moment when Lindsay recalled the script *L* on all Laverne's clothing, because the girl's eyes got big as saucers. "You mean Laverne and Shirley were—" She couldn't bring herself to say the word again. Bailey gave her a big grin. "Oh, my God!" Lindsay shouted, squinting hard, trying to get the image of Laverne and Shirley doing a 69 on each other out of her head. "I had no idea! And I used to watch the reruns of that show every night!" the youngster said, grossed out as though this horrid condition might have come through the airwaves and rubbed off on her.

Bailey gave her a savvy wink. "Live and learn, kid...live and learn," she said as she bit into her bagel heartily. Yeah, learn to tell when someone is zoomin' you...ya friggin' moron.

❧

The first Thursday in February, Bailey walked in shortly after 10 o'clock and immediately noticed something awry. "Where's Lindsay?" she asked, seeing the vacant chair.

"She's been sick all week with the flu," Max replied.

"Jesus, I'm not surprised," she said, putting her jacket back on. "It's freezing in here."

"Something's wrong with the heat in my office and maintenance can't come until tomorrow," Max explained.

"Well, let's move to my office today—I can't work like this," Bailey said, then led the writers down the hall.

Bailey took her seat. "Jeez, Lindsey must have it pretty bad if she's been out all week. Have you sent her flowers or anything?" she asked Max.

He looked puzzled. "No...you think I should?"

Bailey sighed. "You're such a guy, Max. Yes, I think you should send her flowers. You know how yucky you feel when you're sick—flowers really perk you up and make you feel better."

He shrugged. "I suppose."

Bailey instructed him to have Wanda take care of the flowers, then opened her notebook. "Okay, today we're working on the scene where Binaca fires her executive editor, Helvetica Black, after she's caught embezzling from the paper. Now, what can we have her say to start the show with a bang?"

Max had an idea and opened his mouth to speak, but instead of his voice, everyone heard the sound of pure anger echoing up from the set below: "What the bloody hell is *this*?"

It was unmistakably Morgan's voice.

The first thing Bailey thought was, for a small woman, Morgan sure had a powerful set of lungs. But before that thought was even finished, the sound of pounding footsteps came booming up the stairs, louder and louder. Bailey cowered in her chair for a moment—until her primal "fight or flight" instinct kicked in. But no sooner had she grabbed the armrests for liftoff to beat a hasty retreat than Morgan, dressed in a stunning emerald green Dior suit, planted herself in the doorway, legs straddled, foiling any getaway attempt.

"What the hell is this?" she shouted at Bailey, holding high in her right hand a rolled-up script. Before the writer could open her mouth to reply, the actress screamed, "Ace *kisses* Binaca?"

Bailey held up her hands to quell Morgan's anger as she stood, preparing to explain, but when she looked up, Morgan had lowered the script, pointing it directly at her. One of Morgan's lapis-blue eyes was closed and the other squinted, like a shooter taking a bead on a target. The expression on her face stirred a fear deep within Bailey that paralyzed her brain, causing her to freeze.

"If this story line is going where I think it's going, you'd best make peace with your god, 'cause you *die!*" she shouted, hurling the script at Bailey as though she were a bad dog. The big woman ducked, and the script went flying over her head and splattered against the wall, falling to the floor in a mangled mess.

The others took this as their cue to hit the road and scurried out the door, but they hung around at Wanda's desk so as not to miss anything good. Bailey figured the flying script was the denouement of the scene and relaxed, but Morgan came charging at her, causing the writer to sprint to the other side of the room, seeking the protection of her desk, with the spunky little woman hot on her heels.

"All right, now, calm down, Morgan," Bailey said in soothing tones as she rolled her executive leather chair in-between herself and Morgan to impede the actress, then continued around the periphery of the room.

"You're planning a *wedding* for my grand finale, aren't you?" Morgan screamed, pushing the chair aside with her foot.

Bailey hopped over a stack of scripts on the floor underneath the windows. "Well, weddings are—"

"And before two people get married, they usually *date* a lot!" Morgan said, kicking over the stacked scripts and charging through.

Bailey slithered along the small space between the large hanging storyboard and the conference table, taking care not to erase any of the writing with the back of her shirt. "Naturally two people—"

"Which means they'll be *kissing* a lot!" Morgan was so much tinier than Bailey, she didn't have to squeeze between the board and the table and made up lost seconds when she rounded the conference table.

Bailey caught a glimpse of Morgan gaining on her and kicked it into high gear, pulling out each chair from the conference table after she passed, throwing up a series of roadblocks. "Usually a couple—"

"And *touching* each other!" Morgan shouted, pushing each chair back against the table so she could pass.

"Well, in some—" Bailey suddenly discovered she was now cornered on the far side of the conference table, because one of the shorter bookshelves had been moved there to stack scripts on and was now blocking her in. As a last resort, she grabbed the nearest chair and put it between herself and Morgan, holding it in place as a barricade.

Morgan crawled onto the chair on her knees, trying to get as close to Bailey as possible. "I've seen this show, you know!" she shouted, wagging a finger under Bailey's nose. "I know what goes on in these bedroom scenes—actors naked together in bed...buns and boobs falling out all over satin sheets...huffing and puffing, grabbing and groping—"

Bailey noticed the small crowd that had gathered outside her office and motioned frantically for Wanda to close the door. To the disappointment of the spectators, Wanda obeyed her boss.

"If you think for one second I'm going to let that graying, greasy putz of a playboy touch me in *any* way, you'd better think again, little missy!" Morgan was reaching as far as she could over the chair and practically had her angry index finger up Bailey's nostril.

The head writer figured she'd better show some backbone and get the upper hand quickly if she was ever going to get out of this one. "Look," she said in a diplomatic yet very firm tone, "I know you and Derek don't get along, but this is business...this is acting, and that's what you've been hired to do."

Morgan hopped to her feet, thrust her hands onto her hips and threw back her head, laughing boldly in a gesture of defiance and strength, and to Bailey, the petite actress looked as big as the Jolly Green Giant at that moment. "So what are they gonna do if I refuse—fire me?" Morgan taunted.

When Bailey couldn't come up with a response, Morgan knew she had won this one and stormed triumphantly toward the door. "You better come up with something else...and quick!" she shouted. When she opened the door, half the pyramid of people with their ears pressed against it tumbled into the room; the other half jumped back, feigning innocence and quickly dispersing as Morgan steamrolled through.

Once everyone had taken their seats again, not uttering a word in the process, Bailey sat down quietly. "Howz about we do a quick rewrite on Binaca's kissing scene with Ace for today's show?" she said, reeking from the stench of defeat.

࿐

That afternoon Bailey was in her office finishing up the work they should have completed that day when she heard a dreamy, masculine voice waft across the room. "Hi, Bailey...got a minute?"

Just the sound of that voice reduced Bailey to a puddle of hormones, and when she looked up and saw Mitch standing in the doorway, a girlish grin involuntarily shot across her face.

Mitch Carrington stood 6 foot 4 and had a body of 220 pounds of bulging, perfectly sculpted muscle. His dark, alluring eyes and perfect face were framed by straight, thick black hair cut in the all-American boy style—short, parted on the side, and short sideburns.

His face and body screamed *sex* unlike any man Bailey had ever seen. Mitch was 24, in the prime of manhood, and exuded an intense aura of machismo and a charisma that was almost enough to make a girl like her consider switching teams...at least for one lustful, passionate inning or two. So it was no coincidence that Bailey was constantly putting Beauregard Buchanan into situations that called for him to be seen in various degrees of undress. After all, why deprive the show's multitude of female fans of a fantasy or two? It was all for the good of the show, of course.

"Sure, Mitch, come on in," she said, motioning for him to take the chair across from her desk.

"How's it going?" he asked as he sat down.

Bailey could tell by the detached look in his eye this was just small talk, a courtesy greeting—he definitely had something specific on his mind, something important enough to pay her a visit in her office for the first time. She returned the pleasantry and asked how he was doing.

"Fine...fine," he replied. "Everything's going great."

Bailey nodded. "Good...good."

An awkward silence fell upon the room. And lingered.

"So...how did the taping go today?" she asked, trying to jump-start this dead-in-the-road conversation.

"Great...great. Beau was seduced by Aruba at his bachelor party."

Bailey remembered the episode. "Ah...when Aruba hijacks the stripper and pops out of the giant cake herself."

"Yep...yep."

The way he sat there smiling reminded Bailey of the Eric Lindros bobblehead she'd gotten last year at a Rangers game, with hands clasped and resting on his lap like a well-mannered little boy. This was so *not* Mitch Carrington. What the hell was this guy up to? Bailey was dying to know what he wanted bad enough to behave, because Mitch flirted with every woman he came into contact with, including herself. She knew it wasn't because she was his type or anything—it was because that was how Mitch was. He was a flirt—a seducer. It was simply his nature to conquer every woman he came into contact with, regardless of what level it was on—whether it was a sexual conquest or simply winning a woman over and making her drool over him. And it was easy to see how he won so often.

Finally Bailey decided to get to the point. "Can I do something for you?"

His fingers clenched and unclenched, and he wet his lips twice with his tongue as if that would lubricate them and allow the words to come out more easily. Just when Bailey thought he was about to speak, Wanda leaned into the room. "Morgan just called—she wants you to come to her dressing room to talk about something." Mitch jumped in his seat when he heard the voice and became slightly distraught, as though he'd been caught at something.

Bailey's eyes rolled back in her head. "Fine," she said, then gestured to Mitch, "as soon as I take care of—"

"Uh, we're done here," he said, hastily getting up and extending his hand to shake hers. "I just wanted to say thanks for writing such a great show today—it was really great. Great show." He shook Bailey's hand so hard her tiny breasts actually bounced under her shirt, and then he was gone.

Wanda's wrinkled brow indicated she was curious as to what he had wanted, but Bailey just shrugged her shoulders to say she didn't have a clue. Then she too stood to go talk to Morgan. But after taking two steps, she stopped. A moment later, she sat back down and picked up the phone.

"Wanda, call Morgan and have her come up to my office."

After a long pause, Wanda said she would. They both knew the pause was because Morgan wouldn't like this power play Bailey was making. Regardless, Bailey knew it was necessary to keep the upper hand in this situation and hold this meeting on her own turf—the home field advantage.

⁊⁊

Before long, Morgan came in, all smiles; but she was, after all, an actress, and Bailey was certain it wasn't genuine. The actress took the seat at Bailey's desk, and the head writer folded her hands decisively on top of it. "Here's the way it's going to be," Bailey stated. "The wedding stays, because weddings are always a big ratings grabber, *but* I'll leave out the kiss."

Morgan steepled her fingers in a gesture of superiority. "And how are you going to manage that?"

"As Ace and Binaca say their vows, Binaca breaks down and runs off in anguish because she's battling something horrible from her past that won't allow her to go through with the marriage."

An eyebrow went up. "Interesting. What?"

Bailey shrugged. "Don't know yet. But I've got plenty of time to come up with something vile and disgusting. Anyway, it saves you from having to do a close-up kiss at the altar. But you know that Ace and Binaca are going to be dating hot and heavy for the three months leading up to the wedding, and sooner or later you two are going to have to kiss. This isn't an arranged marriage—people in America just don't marry someone they haven't kissed. It would be insulting to our audience to try to pull that off."

Morgan cocked her head in defeat. "I suppose with creative camera angels and concealing lighting we could get around an actual kiss in those scenes."

Bailey smiled. "I'll tell Blaine to shoot one of you from the back of the head so your lips don't actually have to be touching. But I don't know how long that will work. So just prepare yourself, because sometime, somewhere in the near future, you may have to actually kiss Derek Young."

A shiver went up Morgan's spine. "Never again!" she shouted defiantly, then got up to walk off the nausea. When she had made a full circle and was headed back to her chair, she saw the shock on Bailey's face. Her blue eyes showed her embarrassment. Well, now that she had let *that* cat out of the bag, she might as well confess.

"A few weeks after I started on the show, he took me to the opera," she explained as she took her seat again. "Apparently he's some big opera aficionado—I think one of his parents was on the board of the New York City Opera back in the '50s or '60s. Anyway, he invited me to the Met to see *Tosca,* which is one of my favorite operas, so naturally I accepted." She paused, then shook her head slowly, indicating what a huge mistake that had been.

"Not exactly the suave Ace Atkinson in real life, huh?" Bailey said, trying hard not to giggle.

"He's a borderline alcoholic, he showed up sloshed to the gills, reeking of gin, then at the interval he had his glass of champagne *and* mine. Then, in the limo on the way home after a late supper, I hear him scoot across the seat, and the next thing I know he's got his tongue down my throat, stinking of mint breath spray and garlic bread!" Morgan grimaced at the recollection.

"Sounds like a pretty awful evening," Bailey said sympathetically.

"You know," Morgan said, "I think what bothered me even more than the stealth kiss was the fact that he sat through the whole performance explaining to me what was going on, just because it was in Italian—like because I had been a child actor tutored on the set instead of in a private school like him that I'm so uneducated I've never heard the story of Tosca!" Again, she was on her feet pacing off her anger. Then a wicked laugh escaped. "Oh, how I envied little Tosca that night. At least she got to commit suicide so she didn't have to be groped and grabbed by the disgusting lech who was constantly trying to get in her pants."

Bailey knew by the abrupt halt in Morgan's pacing

that she had let that juicy tidbit slip out too. But the way Morgan was standing to the side, wearing a custom-tailored suit that emphasized her famous D-cup breasts, Bailey could easily understand how Derek had been tempted to touch. The actress tried to cover her gaffe by quickly laughing it off. "Perhaps you could work that in somehow—suicides are big ratings grabbers too," she said, then hurried out of the room.

Bailey felt Morgan's suggestion was only half serious, but still there was a little venom in her voice, as though she wasn't too pleased with Bailey's idea for the finale. But she knew actors were temperamental creatures, so she let it slide.

However, after a few minutes, the wheels began churning in Bailey's brain. "A suicide at a wedding," she pondered aloud. "Hmmmm...a double whammy finale."

That little seed began sprouting, and Bailey started jotting down notes for working up a climactic suicide scene for Binaca's farewell performance. She still had almost three months to go until the May 5 finale and was certain she could flesh out a slam-bang show in that time.

Chapter Nine

"Have you seen this?!"

Mike Mahoney tossed the latest issue of *Soap Opera Digest* on top of the papers Bailey was working on when he barged in late Monday afternoon. The screaming headline at the top of the magazine's cover read BINACA TO GET KNOCKED OFF??? SAY IT ISN'T SO!!!

"Who leaked this?" he bellowed. "Our story lines are supposed to be strictly confidential!"

"Why are you screaming at me?" Bailey shouted back, rising from her chair to get to an equal vantage point. "You think that I, of all people, don't know that?" She opened the magazine and flipped to the article, scanning it for a source.

"Don't bother," Mike yelled. "I already checked— the quote is from 'an anonymous source,'" he said in a smarmy tone.

Bailey gave him a "gimme a break" look.

"I'm sorry," he said, rubbing his forehead, trying to

calm down, "it's just that this was supposed to be a big secret so it would all be a great surprise to the viewers on Morgan's last episode. Now the suspense is gone and our ratings are going to go flat!"

"Maybe not," she replied encouragingly. "Maybe all the publicity will get more people interested. Remember what happened with that 'Who shot J.R.?' thing on *Dallas*—that was what put that show on the map."

"Yeah, but that was because the damn tabloids didn't blow the surprise about who the killer was!" he shouted, becoming agitated once again. "Our big secret is already out, and this is only the first week of February—we're still three months away! Jesus Christ," he grumbled. "When I find out who leaked this, I'm firing his ass!"

Bailey could only hope it was Lindsay, but then she remembered Lindsay had been out with the flu the previous week and probably wasn't in the proper frame of mind to be blabbing top secret information to an entertainment journalist. "I'll round up the writers tomorrow and make inquiries," she offered.

"You do that!" Mike shouted, then stormed out, slamming Bailey's door behind him.

Three days later when Bailey met with the dialogue writers, she was surprised to see Lindsay's chair vacant for the second week in a row. Max said the newcomer had called to say she'd gotten out of the hospital on Monday and would try to come in toward the end of the week.

"What?" Phillip said. "You mean she dialed the phone all by herself?" The others snickered.

"Jesus," Bailey said, with great concern, "I didn't know she'd been *that* sick. Well, tell her not to push herself—we don't want her having a relapse."

"Yeah, and we don't want Typhoid Mary spreading her germs around, getting the rest of us sick, either," Stephano added with a frown.

While everyone settled in, the topic of where to go for lunch came up, because Max had missed breakfast and was already starving. "Let's do lunch at the Fashion Cafe," Rhonda suggested.

"Didn't that place go under a couple of years ago?" Phillip said.

Bailey snorted a laugh. "Well, what do you expect from a restaurant where the blue plate special was a Tic Tac?"

The others cracked up, and Phillip said, "And all for only 50 bucks!"

After general grousing about all the over-priced theme restaurants in the city, Suzette smiled, looking at their head writer. "Speaking of high fashion, Peter said Bailey bought an Armani suit at Bergdorf's," she said in a tattletale tone.

All instantly became bug-eyed, like she was hotsy totsy or something for shopping at Bergdorf's, which embarrassed the boss. "I had only planned on taking it for a test drive, but it didn't quite work out that way," she said in her own defense, then began the tale of her disastrous shopping spree a while back for her big date.

She had gotten to the part in her tale where the

snooty salesgirl who needed the hip replacement was trying to run away when the office door was pushed open in a clamor and in hobbled Lindsay on crutches, her left leg in a cast up to her knee. "Sorry I'm late," she said sweetly, "but it's a little difficult getting around with this thing, as I'm sure you can imagine."

Max dutifully sprang from his seat and busied himself with helping the young girl cross the room, taking her purse and leather monogrammed lunch bag. But Bailey sat, teeth grinding, feeling like the biggest sap in a Vermont forest. Her eyes went around the table, seeing the identical expression on the other faces sitting with her. They all knew what had happened too and couldn't wait to see how the girl was going to try to worm her way out of this one.

Lindsay took her seat and grabbed a pencil and paper from her purse as if she were ready to go. "So, what are we working on today?" she said, without a hint of nasal congestion.

Rhonda replied, "Bailey was telling us about jousting with the bitches at Bergdorf's when she bought her new suit."

"Oh—they can be monsters, can't they?" she said to Bailey as if the two were best buddies. "I bought a beaded Dolce & Gabbana for our spring formal last year, and when I got it home, I found *three beads* missing from the pattern in the back. Well, I couldn't wear this defective garment—I would have been the laughing stock of the Greek community. So I took it back and got my money back!" she boasted. "Well, no one in the house could believe it, and after that, I was known as the Rosa Parks of Greek row," she bragged, absolutely beaming with pride.

Everyone was flabbergasted by the comparison. Once they regained their senses, they readied pencils and paper, but Bailey wasn't quite ready to get down to business. "I've never heard of the flu causing a broken leg before...did you take a tumble out of bed?" she asked, looking at the plaster cast.

A momentary flash of panic reflected in the girl's face—just a slight change in the focus of her eyes; the tiniest drop in the corners of her smiling mouth. But apparently she had come well-rehearsed, and she dived right in to her explanation.

"No, actually, I slipped in the shower," she said, shrugging her shoulders as if she were embarrassed about what a big klutz she was. "Yeah, I was pretty out of it from all the antihistamines and aspirin—my doctor said it could have been that combining too many cold medications just made me a little woozy and out of it."

Max was quick to chime in. "You know, that sort of thing happens all the time," he said, just a little too exuberantly. "I mean, all those over-the-counter medications have warnings about mixing drugs and drug interactions. You have to be real careful."

Bailey noticed the sweat mustache that had formed on Max's upper lip, which told her he was as guilty as Lindsay. If she hadn't known for a fact that he'd been at work every day, she would have suspected him of being off with the child at some ski lodge roasting his nuts in front of a blazing fire. Nevertheless, she now knew she was going to have to punish Max in some way too for allowing Lindsay to go on her little ski trip. And she was angry at him for putting her in this situation, not to mention the fact that he'd tried to pull something so lame and poorly contrived over on her.

She had to decide whether to call them on their charade now or let it go until after the meeting, when the rest of the staff had been dismissed. She figured it wouldn't hurt to make the pair suffer a little more before getting on with the meeting. "So who was your doctor?" Bailey inquired.

The question took Lindsay by surprise. Her eyes darted over to Max for help, instinctively, but of course, there as nothing he could do. "Why?" she said.

"Because Wanda will probably need to help you with your insurance claim forms, et cetera, and she'll need all that information...and your receipts from the hospital, your office calls, your medications."

"Oh...well...I'll—I'll have to dig them out. I've been so out of it I really don't remember where I put them. In fact," she said, tapping a finger on her chin as though deep in thought, "I don't even know if I got receipts, to tell you the truth."

Bailey couldn't help smiling. The truth. From this girl? Now, that would be novel. "I'll tell you what," she said, "I'll come over this evening and help you round up all those items. I'm sure you could use the help."

"No! Uh, that's all right. My place is such a mess, you know, I haven't felt like cleaning it up in two weeks so...thanks, but I'll look for them this weekend."

But Bailey wasn't done yet. "I don't mind. I'd really

like to try to find those receipts, 'cause to tell *you* the truth," she said, locking eyes with Lindsay, "I've been genuinely concerned for your well being the last two weeks." Lindsay's eyes lowered. "By the way, did you get the flowers I had Wanda send you last week?" A quick twist of the knife.

The guilt Bailey dished out didn't have much effect, though. "Why, yes, I did," Lindsay beamed. "They were lovely." When it was obvious Bailey wasn't going to be able to guilt a confession out of the girl, she turned her attentions back to the day's business.

౭ఆ

The following day Bailey had lunch with Peter in her office and caught him up on the latest dish on Lindsay. He asked his boss how she was going to punish her, but Bailey didn't know.

"I'd like to fire her; that's what I'd like to do. You won't believe the dialogue that moron writes," she said, then got up and retrieved yesterday's script, which she'd been polishing up before lunch. She opened it to a specific page. "Look at this—*look* at this!" she shouted, holding the script down for him to see, slapping the page with the fingers of her left hand at the selected passage.

Peter burst out laughing. "'A roaring borealis?' What does she think it is, the same thing as a roaring fire only in the sky?"

"Who knows? And look at this," she shrieked, turning to another page. He read the paragraph Bailey was pointing to. "'It makes you look cheap and tottery?'" he said, giggling hysterically.

"And the *pièce de résistance*," Bailey said with conviction, flipping to another page. "Remember the scene where Blaze Blizzard develops a fear of heights after falling from a tree while rescuing a little girl's kitty, and he goes to see the police psychiatrist?"

"Oh, dear God," Peter said, taking the script out of Bailey's hands to get a closer look at this one, just to make sure his eyes weren't playing tricks on him. "'You did very well on your *Horshach* Test'?" he said, in awe of the girl's stupidity. "I suppose she thinks that was something invented by Dr. Vinnie Barbarino?" He dropped the script onto the table like it was trash he didn't want to dirty his hands with any longer. "You are working with Norm Crosby's demon seed," he concluded. "What are you going to do?"

"I don't know," she said, plopping onto her chair, shaking her head, dazed by frustration, "if she were a horse I could take her out and shoot her." The frazzled writer threw up her hands in defeat and pulled her chair up close to her desk to start on the daily mail, but a knock on the door stopped her. It was Mitch Carrington. For any actor to come see her at all was strange, but for the same one to come see her twice within a week, that was downright suspicious, and she wondered what this man could possibly want from her.

The hunky actor seemed uncomfortable to find someone else in the room, which Peter picked up on immediately and excused himself. When Mitch came in and started up the same old small talk, Bailey knew she had to nip this in the bud. So instead of responding to his trivial questions, she said frankly, "Mitch...I want you to just tell me why you're here today," then she folded her hands atop her desk, keeping her eyes focused on his, and waited for him to speak.

The man turned 10 shades of red before he finally spoke. "There's this girl," he said, sitting in the chair in front of Bailey's desk, then a long pause ensued. But Bailey wasn't about to say anything to give him another opportunity for a diversion, so she continued her silence, which prompted him to speak again. "I've never met anyone like her," he said, with a sparkle in his mahogany brown eyes.

Bailey's only response was to smile, as if to say she was happy for him. But still she didn't have a clue as to where she fit into this picture.

Mitch clasped his hands between his legs, hung his head, and let out a heavy sigh. "I've always used the same old lines just to get a chick in bed," he confessed. "I'm real good at that, I've had so much rehearsal."

Bailey imagined it wouldn't take more than a line or two from this Adonis to get a girl in bed; she didn't doubt him one bit.

"But now I can't talk with this girl. I don't know what to say! And I really like her...in fact, I think I might be in love with her and I don't want to screw things up. So...I was wondering if you would write me some dialogue for a dinner scene."

Bailey could hardly believe her ears.

"I'm taking her to Le Cirque for Valentine's Day—did you know it takes *three months* to get a reservation at that place?" He shook his head in disbelief. "Anyway, I've only got five days to come up with some dialogue, and you seemed like the logical place to go, you being so good with words and all."

"Well, thank you, Mitch, but don't you think it would be better if it were *your* words she heard instead of mine?"

"But that's just it," he said, becoming agitated and standing up to pace, "I can't think of any words! At least not the right ones, so I end up not saying anything at all, and then I get afraid she might think it's because I don't like her, and it's making me crazy!"

Somehow Bailey couldn't help feeling sorry for the guy, being so inept as a lover. "So tell me, what is it about her you like so much?"

His face lit up at the thought. "Oh, gosh...she's beautiful, she's sexy, she's sweet."

Bailey smiled. "Then *tell* her," she said quietly. "It's that simple. And that's just the sort of thing a woman loves to hear, no matter how frilly or how simple the words. Just tell her."

"I can't—I can't! I put my big foot in my mouth and get all tongue-tied. Please do this for me, Bailey!" he pleaded, sliding into the chair again, clasping his hands together in a gesture of desperation. "She might be the one, and I don't want to lose her. Please?!"

At that moment Bailey knew there was a good chance she would end up inheriting the nickname "Slinky" from Sam Ryerson. But damn it, she couldn't help herself. "Sure, Mitch...I'll help you out."

"Oh, thanks, Bailey—you're a doll!" he said, and shook her hand vigorously.

Only moments after he left, Bailey started asking herself why she'd agreed to this asinine request. She didn't have time for garbage like this with all the rewrites piling up, and she still had to come up with Morgan's big finale. Fuck! She just wished Lindsay could have been here to hear that speech—that would surely cure her of this juvenile crush she had on the man.

Suddenly a light bulb went off over Bailey's head.

☙

As the afternoon dialogue session was breaking up around 4 o'clock and the writers were filing out the door, Bailey popped in and asked Lindsay to have a seat back at the table. "I need to speak with you for a moment," she said, which brought a smile to all the other faces except Max's.

The last writer out closed the door so the two could have privacy, and Lindsay hobbled back into her chair. She sat, hands folded, looking sweet and innocent, waiting for Bailey to speak.

"I know that you just started here five weeks ago, and that isn't really a lot of time to get adjusted to the way we do things around here..."

Lindsay was sure she was going to get busted. Her heart pounded and her palms went sweaty.

"So it may come as a shock to you that I've decided to give you a special assignment to work on instead of your regular duties."

She couldn't believe her ears. "Really?"

"Yes. Mitch Carrington needs someone to help him with some dialogue for an extracurricular project, and I've decided to give that assignment to you."

Lindsay responded in typical Hanna-Barbera fashion: eyes telescoping from their sockets...tongue unfurling across the table...heart pounding a foot beyond her rib cage.

"You'll be spending a lot of evening hours with him working on this because he's busy with the show during the day."

Lindsay's face bore the expression of a woman on the verge of orgasm. "I don't mind," she said dreamily.

Bailey glanced at the plaster cast on Lindsay's leg and shook her head. "On second thought, I shouldn't be asking this of you now—not with your leg in a cast. That has to be painful and distracting. I shouldn't impose on you," she said, then stood up and gathered her things as if she were leaving.

Lindsay grabbed her boss by the sleeve with both hands. "I'm fine! Honestly! And it's not that painful anymore since the swelling has gone down. Really—I want to do this. I *insist* on taking this assignment," she said bravely.

Bailey admired her for a moment. "You got it," she said with a smirk.

∗

Back in her office, Bailey was taking a moment to gloat over her manipulation of the airhead. This new arrangement would certainly be no hardship to the writing staff—after all, it wasn't like Lindsay had been hired to be a contributing factor. This was just Daddy pulling a few strings so his spoiled little brat could have one more thing she wanted served up on a silver platter.

Bailey was in the middle of clearing out the rest of the mail in her in basket before the weekend when she opened a letter that made her smile disappear. It was from an angry fan who was quite upset over hearing of Morgan's impending ouster from the show. The letter didn't concern Bailey, because the writers occasionally got mail sent directly to them, since their names appeared on the credits at the end of each show. And this letter started out like all the rest, bitching and moaning about things that were happening on the program. But it ended in what Bailey thought was a somewhat bolder manner than the others: The letter writer said that if they didn't keep Morgan on the show, they would regret it.

It bothered her a little, then she realized it was easy to mistake the emotions in written words, so she blew it off. So the ratings would dip a millionth of a point if this bozo tuned out. Who cared?

It was signed "An Angry Fan." Coward, Bailey thought as she tossed the letter aside. No guts, no balls.

Chapter Ten

"Okay, I've got someone much more tame for you this time," Peter said, determined to play matchmaker for Bailey once again. "She's new to the club, so I doubt she'll ravish you on a first date," he said with a giggle.

Alec excused himself from the dinner table when Peter brought out the photo albums and again got cozy in his living room chair, busying himself with finding out what was on Monday night's prime-time lineup.

"Her name is Lorraine Travis," Peter said excitedly. "She's a friend of one of the architects who works with Alec...she works in the law firm on the same floor." He came across a picture of Lorraine from the previous year's Christmas party at Alec's firm and pulled it out.

Bailey cocked her head on first glance, not seeming too excited about the dwarfish woman with the short curly brown hair and round face. "Vital stats, please," she requested as she studied the chick in the photo.

"She's 28...5 foot 1...don't know her weight...married three times...and has six kids."

Bailey was stunned. "Married three times? Six kids? What—does she think I'm a *guy*?!"

"No, that's why she made the switch to our team in the first place. She's tried every form of birth control known to man and finally just got tired of gettin' knocked up."

"That's not a very good track record, Peter. Married three times...with six kids...and she's only 28?"

"So? That just means she's affectionate and likes sex, which should be of interest to you, my dear," he said, wiggling his eyebrows nefariously.

"Yeah, well, I don't know about getting into *that* on the first date anymore. After your last effort at match-making, I'd probably end up in the hospital."

Peter slapped his palms on the table. "What did that woman do to you?" he asked, bursting with curiosity.

Bailey wouldn't look at him. "Nothing," she said innocently.

"Nothing? Honey, you were walking around with three days between your legs—don't tell me *nothing*!"

At that moment they were distracted by Alec's grousing from the living room. "Where do they get this crap?" he moaned, looking at the television guide. "*Ten With Macaroni*? What is that, some movie on the Cooking Channel?"

Peter puffed out a sigh of exasperation before prancing over with heavy footsteps and grabbing the guide away from Alec. After a moment, his hands dropped to his sides and his eyes rolled skyward. "*Tea*

With Mussolini!" he blurted out, then stomped away, shaking his head. "Put yer glasses on!" he shouted back to his blind lover.

When Peter had seated himself next to Bailey again, she handed him back the photo. "She's really not my type," Bailey said, crinkling her nose.

This insulted Peter and what he perceived as his good taste. "What do you mean? You don't even know her!"

"Well...she's not as pretty as Cheyenne, for one thing."

His eyes went rolling around in their sockets. "Obviously! Who is?"

"And she's too short for me. Plus, she looks kinda square—like a schoolmarm. I don't know, she just doesn't do it for me. And I've only had sex once in the last four months, so I was kinda hoping to get hooked up with someone I could get excited about, if you know what I mean."

"So?" he said with a strange grin.

Bailey shrugged, not knowing what he meant.

"Brown bag it," he said.

"What?"

"If things get that far, pull out that mental brown bag and slip it over her head."

Bailey's mouth flew open. "Peter! God, you men are so disgusting!"

"Hey," he said, stacking his albums neatly, "sometimes you gotta do what you gotta do."

"Yeah, well, I ain't gonna be doin' it with her, thanks anyway."

"Oh, come on," he whined, "one lousy date. Who

knows—you may end up liking her, right?"

Bailey refused to admit to the possibility.

"Just take her out to dinner. You'll be in a public place, so you won't have to get all lovey-dovey or anything, and you can have some quiet dinner conversation. It'll be good for you to get out again. It's been a month."

Bailey slumped over, hands dangling between her legs, debating over what to do. Peter wrote down a phone number on the back of the photo and shoved it into Bailey's hands. "Call her...What harm can it do?"

Reluctantly, Bailey stuffed the picture into her shirt pocket.

❧

After she got home, Bailey sat on her bed cross-legged debating this blind date business for a full hour before giving in and calling Lorraine. She finally got around to asking her out for dinner on Wednesday of that week, but she immediately knew she'd made a big mistake when Lorraine got all excited and gushed about what a romantic Valentine's Day dinner the two would have. Bailey had totally forgotten Wednesday was Valentine's Day, when even a simple dinner could be blown all out of proportion just because of that one particular date—February 14. Oh, that cursed date.

As soon as she hung up, she picked up the receiver again and called Lorraine back to reschedule for another day, but the line was busy. No doubt Lorraine was calling her mother telling her about her new

Valentine's Day love. Bailey replaced the receiver in its cradle and fell back against her pillows. Christ, she hated playing the dating game.

❦

Lorraine was definitely no Cheyenne. She was a foot shorter and a foot wider. And the cotton print dress she had chosen made her look like such a plain Jane that Bailey felt overdressed in her Armani suit. But she convinced herself that maybe Lorraine would turn out to be interesting and nice—it was at least worth the price of a dinner and cab fare to find out.

The two introduced themselves and shook hands. "I'm hungrier than a cow," Lorraine proudly announced, "and they have four stomachs!"

Bailey's singular stomach turned queasy. So much for hope.

❦

Rosalie's was the perfect place for their date, Bailey figured, a quaint old-fashioned Italian restaurant in Tribeca where there were only tables and chairs—no booths for scooting together and nuzzling in public or even getting close enough to hold hands under the table. She didn't want her date getting *any* romantic notions tonight.

The menus were already on the table, and they each picked one up and began perusing, which made it seem like there was a reason for the awkward lull in the conversation. A waiter with a white towel tied around his front like an apron approached the table to take their drink orders, and Bailey asked if Lorraine would care for some wine. "You know, I think I will," she said enthusiastically, and Bailey ordered a bottle of good burgundy from the list.

After the waiter left, Lorraine giggled. "It is so nice to be able to have a drink on a dinner date for a change," she said. Before Bailey had time to ask why, the woman blurted out, "I get tipsy after one glass of wine, and since I get pregnant if a guy even looks at me cross-eyed, it just wasn't safe before. But now that I'm dating my own kind, that shouldn't be a problem, huh?"

Bailey's face turned red, and her eyes darted about to see whether anyone around had heard this true confession. Lorraine picked up on her discomfort. "Peter did tell you I have children, didn't he?" she asked.

"Oh, yes," Bailey said, forcing a smile, "six of them."

Lorraine's momentary concern dissipated and she went back to babble mode, talking as though she were in a room of longtime friends instead of strangers. "Believe me, none of them was planned. I took the pill, used foam, a diaphragm, condoms, IUD—you name it, I've tried it. But none of them worked. As a result, I've got a six-pack of kids."

When she hauled her purse up to the table and extracted a wallet full of photos, Bailey wanted to run for the hills. Was there anything more annoying than some stranger going on and on about her passel of kids to someone who obviously didn't have the slightest interest in children?

"This is my oldest, Sarah—she's 8. She was the contraceptive foam that didn't work for shit." Bailey flinched and glanced over her shoulder at the couple behind them, who caught the remark and apparently didn't find it very appetizing. "And this is Raymond, he's 7—the diaphragm disaster," she said, rolling her eyes. "This is Mark, he's 6. Faulty IUD."

Bailey was thankful when the waiter returned at that moment with the wine and interrupted the conversation...or so she thought. "I think you're getting the picture as to why I started dating women," Lorraine proclaimed without an ounce of modesty, causing the waiter to give Bailey a quick reflex look. But being a professional, he made no comment, either verbally or facially, and went about his business uncorking the wine.

When he poured the standard half ounce into Bailey's glass for tasting, she wanted to tell him to just hand over the bottle. But she declared the wine palatable, and the waiter poured them each a glass and departed again.

Bailey picked up the red-and-white checkered napkin from the table and spread it out completely over her lap—to protect her suit as much as possible—then asked Lorraine about her job. The diversion worked until their dinners arrived, when Lorraine immediately fell back into Mommy mode.

"I *hate* being pregnant!" she groused. "My boobs swell up so big I have to sleep with a nursing bra on the whole nine months just to keep them from sloshing from side to side, and they hurt like hell! Before, my breasts were like two firm Jell-O molds, but after the first baby...well, you know what Jell-O's like after it's been left out for four hours?"

Bailey had just sucked up a mouthful of her side order of spaghetti, and it was all she could do to swallow the gooshy noodles at that moment. Her writer's brain kicked into high gear to come up with several topics to get this woman to shut up about this stuff, but she waited too long and Lorraine was running freely at the mouth again.

"And my *gut*—oh! They never tell you about what pregnancy does to your abdomen," she said, pushing in on her belly. Bailey sat back and almost gagged. "Nothing but mush," the woman lamented. "Like a gunnysack full of mashed potatoes. And you should see the scars! My tits look like road maps. Wanna see?"

Bailey almost came out of her chair, and Lorraine giggled flirtatiously. "Well, maybe later," she said, raising an eyebrow seductively. "Anyway, with me being five-foot-nothing, the first little bugger started tearing her way out during the birth, so I had to have an episiotomy. And just my luck, I got stuck with Dr. Zorro—*phfft! phfft! phfft!*" she said, making three strokes of the letter *Z* with her steak knife. "You wouldn't *believe* the scar that bastard left me with."

Bailey's crotch puckered up so tight she felt certain she would have to be pried loose from her chair to break the suction when it came time to leave. She had to stop chewing and sit for a moment, looking like a chipmunk, waiting for her throat to unclench. Did this woman have no sense of decorum? Bailey looked forward to receiving an engraved invitation to Lorraine's next pelvic exam.

≈

Briefly, Bailey considered not even getting out of the cab to walk Lorraine into her building, but that was just too rude—despite her extreme disappointment at how the date had gone, she couldn't be that much of a cad. So she paid the cabbie and figured since she'd already endured two hours of hell, she could manage another 10 minutes to walk Lorraine to her door and say good night properly.

When they opened the door to the apartment, the two were hit by a wave of A&D Ointment, popcorn, shrill voices screaming, and a high school–aged baby-sitter with a belly-button ring as she carried a crying baby with a loaded diaper. She anxiously dropped the kid into Lorraine's hands while demanding payment right then and there, adding that she'd *never* sit for these mongrels again.

Lorraine turned to Bailey with pleading eyes, holding out the screaming infant for her to take so Lorraine could free up her hands and get to her purse. Reluctantly, Bailey took the handoff and held the baby on her hip. But after getting a whiff of the stink wafting up, she held the kid out like it was a bomb that had already gone off. That was all she needed—to get baby poop on her good suit.

When the baby-sitter had left, Bailey returned the

child to its mother, but just as she heaved a sigh of relief, a small child ambushed her from behind, grabbing her around the thighs. "You got a big butt!" the tiny boy announced proudly.

Bailey turned red, then turned around to see what had leeched onto her, but the kid had his head planted firmly between her thighs and she couldn't see anything but a pair of Star Wars jammies. His mother told the child to let go, and he obeyed, much to Bailey's relief, but the brat left a clear set of tan fingerprints on her pants that the NYPD would kill for...if they could manage to get that tape they used to work on peanut butter. So much for a clean getaway.

Lorraine saw the damage and gave Bailey a smile that was both pathetic and proud at the same time. "That's Danny...he's 4," she said as the rest of her brood rushed them. "He's my little Greek tragedy," she added, then leaned over to whisper something to Bailey, who really didn't want to hear about some one-night stand with a guy from Greece. "The Trojan broke," Lorraine confessed in a heavy whisper. Bailey wanted to hear about *that* even less and turned away feeling quite embarrassed at Mom talking about sex right in front of the kids. All the kids. All six of the kids. What the hell had she been thinking when she agreed to this?

"Come on," Lorraine said to her date, nodding toward the hallway as she patted her baby on the bottom, "I'll get you both out of your dirty pants," she said in what Bailey considered a pathetic attempt at maternal humor.

It was on their way down the hall that Bailey began to understand why she always saw mothers in grocery stores letting their kids run wild, screaming like banshees through the aisles. It was because with kids, the noise never stops, and apparently mothers learn to tune out the children in order to save their hearing and their sanity.

At the changing table in the nursery that also housed bunk beds for two other vermin, Bailey was given a box of Handi Wipes and she began dabbing carefully at the peanut butter fingerprints. Lorraine laid the baby on the table and efficiently got to work. "Why don't you slip out of those," she suggested "A little seltzer will take that out in a jiff."

A *jiff*? Was that supposed to be funny too? This woman's sense of humor was really grating on Bailey's nerves. "I'd rather not," she responded as she continued wiping at her pants. "It might seem funny to the neighbors—first date and she's taking her clothes off in front of the little ones," she said, giving up the attempt since she was only smearing the oily foodstuff around, making it worse. A good dry cleaner was the only solution to this problem.

The reeking diaper was deposited into a plastic pail, and while Lorraine wrestled with the squirming kid and a new, uncooperative diaper that wouldn't unfold, Bailey looked around the room at toys and stuffed animals. A cute wooden train engine with wheels that looked like peppermint starburst candies with red-and-white stripes around the edges caught her attention, so she picked it up. She spun one of the peppermint wheels a couple of times before checking out the toy to see what else it did. When she turned it upside down, the CAUTION label caught her eye. *"Wheels are not real candy—do not attempt to eat,"* she read aloud, then puffed out a sarcastic laugh, recalling the warning label on the hair dryer she'd just bought that actually said: DO NOT USE WHEN ASLEEP. "What kind of moron would be that stupid?" she said absentmindedly.

Lorraine, who was holding two adhesive tabs in her mouth while positioning the clean diaper on the baby, freed one hand long enough to grab the tabs. "Sarah, honey!" she shouted "Come tell Auntie Bailey about the time you gave Mommy the Heimlich maneuver!"

Bailey quickly put the toy down. "You know, maybe I should go," she said, backing toward the door, "it looks like you're going to have your hands full for the rest of the night."

Instead of being disappointed, Lorraine smiled. "Actually, I was hoping to get my hands full of something else tonight," she said, aiming at provocative but missing by a mile.

When Sarah charged in, Lorraine handed the freshly changed baby to her and instructed the girl to take the other children into her bedroom and pick out a bedtime story to read them so Mommy and Bailey could have some privacy for a little while.

Bailey took a seat on the living room couch while Sarah rounded up the herd, and Lorraine went out to the kitchen to make them a drink. Soon the Von Trapp Children began filing past Bailey, heading off to bed, thank God. So long, Sarah. Farewell, Raymond. Auf wiedersehen, Mark. Good night, whatever your name is—in all the commotion she had not been introduced to the baby in Sarah's arms or the other toddler, still in diapers, who was now waddling by.

At the end of the line, Danny boy was bringing up the rear. Bailey's brown eyes locked onto the little urchin. Big ass, huh? Ruin my $4,000 suit, will ya? She hated little Danny.

When the boy was directly in front of Bailey, her psyche took a warp-speed journey back to childhood, resulting in a reflex reaction that made her right leg kick straight out. The kid hit the deck like a sack of wet cement.

Danny did a push-up to his knees and first checked his hands for injuries. Then he shot hatred darts at Bailey as he got to his feet. She tossed the darts right back, only hers were accompanied by a smile of supremacy, because they both knew the score—they both knew that in Kidworld the rules say that if a kid tries to blame something on an adult, the adult always wins. Tattling would be hopeless. So Danny took it like a man and didn't say a word; he just turned now and then on his way to the bedroom to plink a few more impotent darts back at Bailey until he got to the door, where in one last gesture of redemption, he stuck out his tongue at the mean lady just before shutting the door.

Suddenly the lights dimmed, which made Bailey jump. She was afraid she had been caught roughing up the kid by his mother, who came in carrying two glasses of red wine. Lorraine sat down right next to Bailey, who quickly got to her feet and went across the room, pretending to browse the bookshelves on the other side of the room. "Nice collection," she said at the rows and rows of books.

"Yes, I think books are so decorative," Lorraine said in all seriousness.

Decorative? Books are decorative? "But I would think that as an attorney, you would have a great appreciation for good literature."

"Oh, I'm not an attorney. I never even went to college," she said, obviously flattered at Bailey's assumption. "I'm the receptionist at the law firm," she explained.

This news flash jostled Bailey's ego. Great. Here she was—an MBA from Harvard—and Peter had set her up with some broad with a high school education whose favorite work of literature was no doubt *The Ice Cream Man Cometh*. Well, it was definitely time to check out. "You know," Bailey said, faking a yawn, "I'm pretty beat myself, so—"

Lorraine sort of slinked over to Bailey and in a breathy voice said, "You know how to fix a yawn, don't you?" She drew closer and closer, eyes focused on Bailey's lips. But instead of taking this for the seduction scene it was intended to be, the writer's brain started churning, and a few seconds later she replied, "With a yanitor?"

Immediately Lorraine began laughing, then she laughed so hard she sloshed her wine, all over Bailey's shoes. After a quick recovery, Lorraine resumed her attack, and just when Bailey thought she'd never escape, they heard a loud bang on the adjoining bedroom wall followed by an ear-piercing shriek. "Mom! Mom!"

The women went rushing into the room, where all six kids were screaming hysterically and crying, but whenever Lisa, the previously unknown toddler, screwed up her face and cried, an arc of blood shot out from a tiny red circle right in the middle of her forehead. Unfortunately for Bailey, she ended up standing in the line of fire, and blood was spurting all over her white shirt and her pants. "Bloody fucking hell!" she shouted, arms spread-eagle at the sight she beheld.

Danny gasped. "Oh! She said a bad word, Mommy!" he shouted, jumping up and down with sheer glee as he pointed a finger at Bailey, so Mom would have no doubt as to who the guilty party was this time.

"What on earth happened?!" Lorraine cried to Sarah, trying to stop the bleeding by putting her hand over the spewing wound.

In hyper-mode, the oldest child puffed out her words: "Lisa was climbing the bookshelf to play with the conch shell we brought back from Florida, only the bookshelf started wobbling like it was going to fall over, and when I pushed it hard against the wall, the shell came falling down and hit her in the head. One of those little spiky things hit her right between the eyes and blood shot out of there like a squirt gun!"

A torrent of blood was seeping through Lorraine's fingers and dripping copiously on the carpet. She yelled at Sarah to run and get a clean diaper, which she quickly placed over the wound and applied pressure. "Oh, my God!" Lorraine wailed, bundling up the bloody child in her arms and swiping her house keys off the dining table as she raced to the door. "Bailey—grab the rest of the kids and meet me downstairs—I'll hail a cab!"

※

The emergency room at St. Vincent's was backed up like the Holland Tunnel on Labor Day, but when the admissions attendant saw two adults and a child all drenched in blood, she hustled Lorraine and the baby in through the doors. Bailey said she'd stay in the waiting room and watch the other kids.

Considering the massive loss of blood, Bailey was surprised when only 40 minutes later Lorraine and Lisa returned with one of the doctors. "Is she all right?" Bailey asked, deeply concerned.

"Yes," the doctor said, patting Lisa gently on the back in her mother's arms, "she's fine. There's a major blood vessel running down the center of the skull between the eyes, and that shell hit the bull's-eye." Then he looked at the round bandage right between the girl's forehead that resembled a round archery target. "No pun intended," he said quickly. "Anyway, it just punctured a blood vessel and not the skull, thank goodness. It looked a lot worse than it was—she was more scared than hurt."

Then he turned to Lorraine and instructed her to keep the girl quiet and home from preschool for a few days, until the scab came off—in order not to reopen the wound.

"Oh, God—I just realized I ran off without my

purse!" Lorraine gasped at the counter, preparing to hand over her co-pay. "It has my insurance card and everything in it," she said, going limp with despair. "I suppose they're going to make me go all the way home and get it, then come all the way back so they can fill out their truckload of forms." Lorraine was so weary by that point she started crying.

Bailey patted her on the shoulder. "I already explained things to them, and because it's so late and you've got all these little ones to put in bed, I gave them your contact information, and they said you could come down tomorrow and take care of it." The news didn't seem to make the weary mother feel any better. "They got your name and address just so you don't try to run out on them," Bailey said, trying to make Lorraine smile again, which succeeded, but only until she remembered she didn't have money for a cab home either. Bailey pulled out all the bills she had left in her wallet and handed the wad of cash to Lorraine. "Here's 20 bucks—that'll cover you."

Lorraine saw the wallet was empty now. "But that's all you've got left," she said, refusing to take the money.

"Take it," Bailey insisted, stuffing the bills into the woman's hands. "I can have someone come and get me. Now get those kids home and into bed—it's way past their bedtime."

Lorraine's lip quivered. "Thanks, Bailey. I would say I've had a wonderful time tonight, but I can't," she said, breaking down again. "Be sure and send me the dry cleaning bill for your suit, okay?"

Bailey gave her a little hug. "Sure, I will," she said,

but of course she had no intention of asking for reimbursement, knowing Lorraine had six better ways to spend that money.

After she put the brood into a cab, Bailey bummed a quarter from one of the waiting wounded and headed to the pay phone at the entrance.

"Hey, Peter...I need you to come get me."

"Again?" he said, part shocked; part perturbed. "Where are you this time?"

"The emergency room at St. Vincent's."

Silence. "You're kidding me," he said, in total disbelief. Bailey sighed. "Come see for yourself."

᠅

Twenty-five minutes later, Peter pulled up to the emergency room entrance, and when Bailey came trudging out looking beat, his mouth fell open at the sight of her white shirt splashed with blood and the dark stains all over her suit. When she sat down next to him, he smelled the wine that had spilled on her shoes and saw the tan smudges on her pants, immediately recognizing the smell of peanut butter. His mouth was still agape when he drove off, but he chose to take a vow of silence and didn't inquire.

Not a word had been spoken by the time they pulled up to a red light several blocks away. With eyes forward, watching the light, waiting for it to change, Peter pursed his lips and tapped a finger on the steering wheel. It was no use—he had to ask. "This doesn't involve any kitchen utensils, does it?"

Chapter Eleven

When Bailey passed by the doorway to the studio after retrieving the day's lunch order from the security desk, she heard a hideous din coming from within. Derek and Morgan were at it again. She scooped up the large, white deli sacks in her arms then took a quick detour to see what was happening.

Bailey went up to Marci at her script podium and was about to ask where Blaine was and why he wasn't in control of his set when something out of the corner of her eye distracted her. There, on the set of Binaca's office, was a man dressed head to toe in a black body-suit on top of Binaca's desk doing a cossack-style dance, squat-kicking alternating legs straight out with arms folded...only he was doing it with a supernatural ease, his feet four inches above the desk top.

"Okay," Bailey said, pointing to the disturbing sight, "I don't remember writing anything about a supernat-ural ninja doing a Russian folk dance on Binaca's desk," she said, glancing over at the man, who was now doing a breaststroke through the ethers.

"It's the Mission Impossible thing," Marci explained.

Ah, that rang a bell. This was the scene where a crooked county commissioner had hired a local ne'er-do-well to break into *The Tribune* offices and steal all the evidence one of the reporters had gathered for a big exposé about him pilfering county funds to pay off personal gambling debts.

"The ropes got stuck on the pulleys while he was lowering down from the skylight," Marci said, stating the obvious.

"Whew—for a moment I thought Blaine had been fired and replaced with David Lynch."

"No, he just had to take a break and went to the john," Marci explained—which instantly made the word "yanitor" pop into Bailey's head, sending a shiver up her spine—"and as soon as he left, these two started in again," Marci continued. "They've been at it *all morning*," she said wearily.

❧

Even with 50 feet and a bathroom door between, Blaine could still hear the ruckus echoing in from the studio. He stood at the urinal, leaning forward with a hand against the wall, impatiently looking over the top of his half-lens reading glasses in order to count the bricks in the wall in an effort to relax enough to make something happen. At last—success.

Suddenly that phlegmy feeling in the back of his throat—which had plagued him all morning since eating a strawberry Pop-Tart for breakfast—acted up again, and he cleared his throat. That didn't work, so he coughed really hard. That did the trick. When he leaned over to spit, his low-slung glasses slid off his nose and landed right on the urinal drain at his feet. Since there was no stopping a man in midstream, all Blaine could do was stand there, pissing on his own glasses, listening to the sound of urine splashing on the lenses. "God-fucking-damn it."

❧

Bailey heard footsteps coming up behind her and turned to see Blaine approaching the script podium. Her mouth had opened, ready to speak, but as soon as she saw him, her jaw dropped completely. Underneath the nose bridge and the earpieces of his glasses was stuffed a square of white toilet paper. With the ends sticking out, flapping as he walked, he looked like some freakish origami bird that was mutating into human form: Definitely a *Twin Peaks* experience.

"Don't say a word," Blaine instructed to no one in particular, as he was avoiding eye contact with everyone, "just call my wife and have her bring down my spare pair," he said, obviously to Marci.

The girl departed posthaste and Blaine leaned wearily on the podium, his head resting atop his folded arms.

"You look like you need a rest," Bailey said.

He found the strength to raise his head. "I need to lie down in a six-foot pine box," he said. "What *is* it with these two?"

"What's the problem today?" she asked.

He started to speak, but Morgan and Derek's voices raged again from her living room set at the far end of the floor. "Well, just listen for yourself," Blaine said, gesturing in their general direction, seemingly delighted that Bailey could witness the disturbance directly from the source.

"This is supposed to be my *home*—why would I hang a mirror so high that I can't see myself in it?" Morgan shouted. One of the two set designers which had ganged up on her along with Derek, who was standing a safe distance back, explained that this was where the eye line of the room was, which caused the actress to go all frothy. "I know I'm short, but do you have to rub it in?!"

"It'll destroy the look of the set," one of the designers said.

"I don't care! I can't see myself in it!" Morgan shrieked as she took off one of her high-heeled shoes and wielded it like a hammer. "*This* is *where* eye-*level* should *be!*" she shouted as she banged the heel over and over on the door frame to mark the spot.

Derek was aghast at the sight. "Holy cow, Khrushchev!" he exclaimed.

Morgan turned her angry gaze on the man. "What? Are you concerned that I'm ruining a $2 piece of wood?"

"No, I'm concerned that you don't pop for a pair of

Odor-Eaters. Good Lord!" He fanned his hand in front of his nose a few times.

Morgan did a slow turn back to face the insolent set decorators. "Once again: The scene calls for me to stop and fix my hair before going in to dinner, at which time I see Drucilla slipping a silver candy dish into her purse because she's suffering from kleptomania. How can I possibly see anything with the damn mirror that high?!"

Derek snorted a laugh and grumbled just loud enough for Morgan to hear, "Yeah, like she has a reflection."

"What did you say?" she shouted at him.

Derek turned to her with a smirk. "What's the matter—your hearing not what it used to be?"

Morgan shoved her hands onto her hips. "Are you trying to say that I'm old?" she said.

He chuckled, speaking to Heather out of the corner of his mouth. "She's so old she learned to write in hieroglyphics."

His nemesis immediately barreled toward him, which caused the others on the set to quickly gather in the far corner for protection. "Look who's talking, Mr. 60 Years Old Next Month!" she said childishly.

Derek put on a front, acting like it didn't bother him to have his age broadcast in front of all these actors who were 30 to 40 years younger. "Well—I'm surprised you can count that high without your abacus." That one cleared the set—everyone dashed to safety, staying close enough, however, that they wouldn't miss the drama.

Morgan folded her arms and threw her head back in a superior fashion. "Look, buster—I'm only a couple of years older than you, so don't act like I'm some medieval creature. For your information, I still have young men drooling after me everywhere I go. How do you explain *that*?" she said, giving him back that smirk.

He paused a moment. "I don't know...maybe they miss their Mommy?"

Morgan's jaw hit the ground amid whistles from the bystanders. But suddenly Derek seemed to have a change of heart and opened his arms in a gesture of reconciliation. "Darling, your age is nothing to be ashamed of. In fact, it's part of what makes you so special. After all, you're probably the only person still living who remembers exactly where she was when President Lincoln was shot."

Morgan squealed with anger and grabbed the first breakable thing within reach, which happened to be a Waterford Crystal egg displayed on the fireplace mantle, which she sent sailing toward Derek's fat head. "For your information," she raged, as the egg crashed to the floor well behind its target, "I've had *dozens* of offers for work—movies, television series, Broadway— I'm *far* from being old and washed up!"

"Well, why switch?" Derek said flippantly. "You should do another soap. You can call it *All My Husbands*. It'll run for *years* with all that material!" he expounded, arms spreading out like a rainbow, inciting Morgan to hasten in search of another prop to throw.

Blaine looked to Bailey with pleading eyes, but this was out of her jurisdiction. She gave him a pat on the back for encouragement and said before departing, "I'll make sure you get a nice, soft lining in that pine box."

❧

"I'm telling you, the woman uses a butt double in all her movies."

This was what greeted Bailey upstairs in her office, where she thought she would be able to get back to a normal world with the breakdown writers. She dropped the white deli sacks on the table and decided not to jump into this conversation just yet.

"No, she doesn't," Evan said vehemently.

"Yes, she does!" Deirdre insisted. "Take a close look at *Pretty Woman* sometime. All the scenes where the camera is panning over her half-nude body—they edit in a cut before they ever show her face. Every time! I'm telling you, the woman has a lard ass!"

Now Bailey knew who they were talking about. And it didn't bother her that the subject was big butts, because she wasn't an actress or a model or trying to be a sex symbol, and they all accepted her for who she was—a middle-aged, pear-shaped woman.

Evan, the only heterosexual male in the room, refused to believe. "That woman is *fine!*" he declared.

Deirdre burst into laughter. "You just rent a copy of *Mystic Pizza*. There ain't nothing mystical about what happened to all the pizzas...they went straight to her *ass*. Seriously. In this one scene, she's wearing a straight skirt and a belt, and it makes her butt look like a shelf.

You could park a breakfast tray on that thing."

The other five around the table cracked up at the shared mental picture. Deirdre was on a roll and as a finale, she stood up to do her rendition of Sir Mix-A-Lot's "Baby Got Back." "I—like—big—*butts,* but I gotta say...Hers is bigger than a Chevrolet!" Hands slapped thighs and the table top as her audience doubled over with laughter. "Got an L.A. face with a big ol' ass!" she sang in finish, then everyone settled down and started distributing the food.

"I'm not even going to ask how you got onto this topic," Bailey said. "How about if we discuss something besides body parts while we eat? Anyone else have anything interesting to talk about?"

Cynthia was about to speak when she, and everyone else, noticed what Bailey was doing with her lunch. The head writer had ordered beef enchiladas, which usually were topped with a red ranchero sauce, but today Bailey had brought her own topping—a can of Hershey's chocolate syrup, which she was now pouring over them.

"Oh, no," LeeAnn said, "Bailey's in a bad mood again today."

Deirdre was horrified when the boss actually took a bite of this mishmash and swallowed. "I'm sorry," she said politely, "I know you're the boss, but I'm going to have to ask you to leave." Everyone knew she was making a joke—they were all used to Bailey's occasional cravings. But Peter was the only one who knew Bailey's ridiculous lunch was directly related to her horrible date last Wednesday with Lorraine.

"Oh, here's something different," Cynthia said. "I got a sort of weird-sounding letter in my mailbox today. "It was complaining about us taking Morgan off the show, but it had a kind of ominous tone to it. I don't know—it just gave me the creeps."

Bailey stopped chewing, remembering the anonymous letter she had gotten. "What did it say exactly?" she asked, trying not to sound concerned.

"I don't remember. I still have it—it's right over there with my other things," she said, nodding toward her purse and notebook on top of one of the bookshelves.

"Let me have it before you leave, okay?" she said nonchalantly.

"Why? Are you worried?"

"No," Bailey replied, which wasn't exactly the truth, "I just want to take a closer look at it. You never know about these things."

≥●.

At 2 o'clock, when the others left, Peter closed the door to Bailey's office. "I didn't want to say anything in front of the others, but I got one of those strange letters today too."

Now Bailey became concerned. "I got one a couple of weeks ago," she confessed. "What did yours say?"

"Here—I kept it to show to you in private. I wasn't sure how you'd want to handle it."

The letter said the writer would be watching the media outlets for news that the show had changed its mind and was keeping Binaca Blaylock. Not a bold threat, but the fact that there were now three of these letters was somewhat disturbing. Bailey looked at the trio of letters on her desk, then placed them in a file and locked it in her side drawer.

⁂

On Thursday, Lindsay's vacant chair once again caused Bailey to ask where she was. Max reminded her that she'd put the girl on some special assignment—but that had been to help Beau with his Valentine's Day dinner, which had taken place last week. "You mean she hasn't showed up all week?" Bailey asked. Max replied to the negative. "I swear to God, that girl is going to do me in," she said. "All right, I'll give her a call this afternoon before I leave and find out what the hell is going on."

She took out her notebook. "Anyway, here's what you need to be working on next. After Aruba seduces Beau, he refuses to break off his engagement with Pashmina, so to deal with her grief and rejection, Aruba sleeps with everything in pants. But after going to England to get away from it all and visit her mother, Myrtle Beach, and her stepsister, Bermuda Schwartz, Aruba becomes ill and goes to the doctor, thinking she might have contracted mad cow disease from eating a steak at the Savoy in London. Instead, she discovers she's pregnant."

Oohs and aahs arose from all around. "Who's the daddy?" Rhonda asked.

"Beau is, but we don't let the audience know that right away—keep 'em guessing and tuning in."

"Um, before we get into this, I wanted to mention something to you," Max said. "A few of us got some strange letters in the mail this week."

A sick feeling hit Bailey. She tried to act like it was no big deal. "Just let me have them when we're through here today, all right?"

But Max could tell she was covering up. "You've gotten some too, haven't you?"

"Just a few, so let's not let our vivid imaginations run wild just yet, okay?" Bailey said authoritatively. "Now, let's get back to Aruba."

Instantly, it was as if Bailey had pushed B-14 on a jukebox. From the writers arose the chorus of "Kokomo" by the Beach Boys. They felt that Bailey should have known better than to leave one like that dangling out there in front of them.

❧

As soon as the dialogue group broke for the day, Bailey went back to her office and called Lindsay at home. She discovered that Beau's dinner had gone so well he asked her to continue writing more dialogue for his dates, and Bailey was thrilled to approve an extension to her assignment.

After she hung up, she felt pretty good. No, she felt great! A tremendous joy began building from within. She had rid herself of this twit in a most clever fashion.

She floated to her feet, stepped atop her chair, then

to the mountaintop of her desk, and let out a wail, a single shrill note carried along on the ethers in a Circe song, proclaiming that all was right in the Land of Soaps once more.

Wanda peeked in to see what the hell was going on, but when she saw it was just Bailey she closed the door behind her and went back to her duties.

❧

By the end of the following week, the two writing staffs had received a total of 47 letters complaining about Morgan leaving the show. Bailey gathered them all up and went to see Mike to report the incident.

"So far none of them has stated an outright threat of harm to anyone," she said, "but with the sheer number and the increasing anger in these letters—I thought it was time to mention it."

Mike was indeed concerned, and he called Stubblefield, who instructed him to notify Nick Peterson, head of network security. Peterson in turn told the producer he would collect the letters and start checking around to see whether anyone else on the show—or any of the network's other shows—had been getting any unusual hate mail. Bailey was instructed to report to Peterson immediately, should she receive any more letters.

Chapter Twelve

A month later, on April 1, the nominees for Daytime Emmys were issued, and Mike asked Bailey to come down to the set as representative of the writers to hear him read off the list. After reading the names of Morgan, Derek, Mitch, and Heather, he said there was one last nomination. "And for best writing, Bailey Connors and her wonderful staff!" he announced, inciting a round of applause, then added, "Without whom none of us would ever have gotten the chance at being nominated in the first place."

Morgan walked over and gave the head writer a big hug. "Congratulations," she said. "If you don't win, there is no justice in this world. You've been phenomenal this year."

"Well, don't get your hopes up," Bailey said modestly, "I've been nominated—excuse me, my *staff* has been nominated—four times in the six years I've been here and we've never won, so..."

"Yes, but that was before you had *me* to write for," the actress said with a wink. "We've done pretty well together, don't you think?"

Bailey couldn't help smiling at having this beautiful woman so close. "I do."

Several others came around and congratulated Bailey personally, then she went up to deliver the good news to her staff.

≥●·

About an hour later, there was a knock at Bailey's closed office door, where the breakdown writers were hard at work. "Who is it?" Bailey shouted, not wanting to be disturbed, since they were on a roll.

"Floral delivery," came the nasally voice through the closed door.

Peter piped up and said, "Candygram!" like Chevy Chase doing the Land Shark skit from the early *SNL* days, which caused the others to snicker.

"Wanda must be on a break," Bailey said, getting up from her chair.

"Don't open it," Peter playfully warned.

Bailey was expecting congratulatory flowers—probably from the network brass—but the FTD delivery man brought in a large standing arrangement of black flowers in the shape of an upside down horseshoe and placed it in the center of the room.

"Black flowers?" she said in disbelief. Then something dawned on her. "I'll bet they're from Bruce Slotzky over at *All My Children*," she said, referring to an acquaintance who didn't get nominated.

Peter's hands went up. "It's an April Fools' joke," he concluded, remembering what day it was. Suddenly his eyes ballooned. "Ooh—gimme the phone, quick!" he said, reaching out with anxious hands. "I want to call Grand Central Station and ask them to page David Mehoff."

"Who's that?" Evan asked, setting the phone on the table.

"No one," Peter replied as he dialed, "but when he doesn't come to the phone, I'll ask them to page his brother, Jack."

Bailey did a spit-laugh on her way out to Wanda's desk to search for a florist's card lying around, perhaps on the floor nearby. When Wanda returned carrying a cup of fresh coffee, Bailey asked if she'd seen the card. "No, but there are *eight more* letters addressed to you that look like that same type font," she said, holding up the morning mail she'd just retrieved.

Bailey opened the first one on the stack, then the second, and the third. When she got to the end of the third letter, her face went visibly pale.

"What is it?" Wanda asked.

Bailey grabbed all the letters and told Wanda to have Peter take over for her, then she headed quickly down the stairs to Mike Mahoney's office.

૨ૹ

Bailey felt like she'd walked into the bull pen of the New York Stock Exchange instead of Mike's office—a dozen of the suits from corporate were buzzing about, shouting offers back and forth across the room, arms waving, bodies pacing. The scene took her by surprise, because these guys never came down from their ivory tower, except to the Monday morning meeting. At first she figured they had already found out about the new batch of letters, but as the flying tidbits of conversation began coming together, Bailey realized this gathering was about something else entirely.

"We can have a contest of some sort and the winners can come see the live show!" someone shouted.

"A contest?" Sam Ryerson said with a smile. "I love it! Live performance—I love that too!"

"Whoa—whoa!" Bailey whispered to Mike, who was caught up in the frenzy and hadn't even noticed her entrance. "Contest winners? What the hell are they talking about?"

"What kind of contest?" Ryerson asked.

The one in the dark pin-striped suit began pacing. "Aruba is knocked up, right, because she's been sleeping around since Beau screwed her at his bachelor party and then didn't break off his engagement to Pashmina...so we make a contest out of who the father is! The first X-number of people who get it right get free admission to the live show."

Ryerson beamed. "Love it!"

"Nationwide or local?" asked Mike.

"Nationwide, of course."

"Are we going to pay for their transportation too?" Ryerson inquired, looking deeply concerned about the dollar signs spinning in his head.

"Hell, no! We don't appreciate the fans that much," Mr. Pinstripe said.

Mike wasn't so sure about this idea. "How many people do you think will travel across the country for this?" he asked.

The suit belted out a laugh. "Have you *seen* the psycho mail we get from these loonie tunes? They *live* for this show. When any two characters get married, they get together with their friends at someone's house and have their own wedding—they do all sorts of weird stuff. Hell, they'll travel halfway around the *world* to see this show," he said confidently.

Bailey nudged her producer. "That's sort of what I need to talk to you about, Mike," she whispered.

"Just a second—just a second," he said, totally blowing her off.

"So where are we going to have the live performance?" Ryerson continued. "The seating capacity will determine how many winners we can pick."

"Mike...I really need to—" Bailey's brain soaked up an important part of the conversation. "What live show?" she asked, sounding a little perturbed and frightened at what the answer might be.

"Radio City Music Hall!" someone chimed in.

Ryerson's eyes zipped over to Morty Feinstein, the show's set designer. "Morty—will that work?" he said with great urgency.

The designer squinted, viewing the location in his head. "It's perfect!" he deduced. "It's got the best-designed stage in the world—a hundred feet wide. It's divided into three sections, each on hydraulic elevators, so we can make *spectacular* sets and effects—we can even get a fountain in there if we want, or make it rain!"

"I don't think we want it raining on Binaca's wedding day," someone said.

The last piece finally fell into place for Bailey. "We're doing Binaca's final show *live?*" she shouted, looking around the room. "What—are you people *nuts?*"

No one paid any attention to the killjoy in the room. Morty continued, "And the orchestra is on another elevator and can be playing from down in the pits until the wedding, when we raise it dramatically!"

"That would make a great visual effect!"

"No, wait—I forgot, they have this huge organ with rooms and rooms full of pipes," Morty said, "We can play the bridal march on it just as if it were a real wedding in a church!"

"Love it!" Ryerson said.

"And the stage also has a huge turntable type thingie to allow quick scene changes from one set to another," Morty added. "And on a live show, we're gonna need quick changes with just four minutes for commercial breaks."

"How many people does Radio City hold?" Ryerson asked.

"Mmmm, around 6,000," Morty replied.

"*Sold!*" Ryerson began tallying up his notes to see what all he had agreed to when Bailey stood and took center stage.

"You guys might want to reconsider the live show when you read this," she said, holding up the letter that was now limp from being mangled in her sweaty hands. Someone asked what it was, and Bailey began explaining about the series of letters the writers had gotten over the last several weeks, in addition to the lovely arrangement of black flowers that had just been delivered to her office. Then she read aloud the letter that had arrived in today's mail so everyone could hear.

"Hope you liked the flowers. We just want to make it clear that if you kill off Binaca, you will be dead to us."

Ryerson held out his hand so he could see the letter himself.

"It's the same handwriting as on a lot of the other letters too," Bailey explained, "but unlike the others, this one says 'us.'"

Ryerson dialed Nick Peterson.

❧

After looking over each letter thoroughly and grilling Bailey for details, Peterson informed Ryerson that he was calling the FBI.

"Aren't you blowing things out of proportion?" Ryerson said. "I think NBS can handle this internally."

Peterson, a short, stocky man whose face indicated that he had no sense of humor, looked Ryerson directly in the eye as he bundled up the letters. "Sir, whenever the U.S. mail is used to make death threats, it's a federal offense," he said in a monotone. "I'm required to notify the FBI, because that's their jurisdiction, and that's exactly what I'm going to do," he said before departing with the evidence in hand.

≿▲

That weekend, Deirdre threw out her back after slipping on her wet kitchen floor, so the following Monday, Bailey had to call Lindsay and bring her back into the fold—the dialogue group simply had to have the extra body. But after lunch on her first day back, Lindsay vomited and went home. Everyone had noted how pale she looked when she came in, and they deduced it was probably some kind of bug or stomach virus.

Lindsay was out that entire week and called in sick the following Monday, and Bailey swore that if the kid came back to work in another cast she would fire the bitch, regardless of the consequences.

≿▲

For Derek's 60th birthday party, one of his friends had thought it would be fun to make the celebration into a roast. One of the ballrooms at the Waldorf had been transformed, with tables set up for 400 friends and associates and, at the front of the room, a dais. Sitting next to the guest of honor at the front of the room was an old and dear friend of his parents, Rowland Price, who had once been a famous Broadway producer.

In his 80s now, Rowland reminisced with Derek about the old days when people dressed to go to the theater and the opera. "Tuxedos...at the very least a suit—no dungarees and sneakers," he said with a snarl. "Women wore gowns and their jewels, and the men showed them off to society. It was a social event, something to be taken seriously. Ah, my, your parents must hate to see all their efforts to enhance the cultural level slip so low. By the way, where are your folks tonight, Derek?"

Derek caught Mr. Price up on his parents, who were too frail to attend tonight's soiree, and he was describing the lovely crystal vase they had sent him to mark the special occasion when out of the corner of his eye he saw big trouble in a red velvet Edith Head gown.

Morgan had not been invited, but no one at the door had guessed as much—after all, she worked with Derek. And anyway, who was going to turn away the great Morgan Gable and cause an embarrassing scene? Everyone but the birthday boy was thrilled when she entered the room.

Periodically during the six-course gourmet dinner, selected friends came up to the dais and took turns delivering clever barbs about the man. After each roaster had finished, Derek graciously shook hands, to show no hard feelings for the skewering. He knew that Daniel Colbert, his college roommate, was the last speaker scheduled, so when Daniel introduced Morgan as a surprise contributor, no one was more surprised than Derek.

She was all decked out in rubies and diamonds to accent her fabulous gown, looking every bit the movie star, and Derek figured this was her way of stealing the spotlight on his special day. Oh, well, she would be out of his life soon enough. Besides, there was always the chance that her jokes would flop and she'd look ridiculous. That thought quickly cheered him up.

Morgan adjusted the microphone for her height. "We all know that Derek comes from a long line of blue-bloods," she said respectfully, which made Derek wonder where the hell she was going with this. "You're the youngest of three brothers, aren't you?" she asked, prompting him to nod in agreement. Morgan grinned, as though a thought had just hit her. "I guess that makes you low man on the scrotum pole."

Spontaneous laughter erupted, and Derek had to force a smile so as not to seem perturbed by the clever jab. Morgan acted surprised he didn't laugh. "What's the matter? A little uptight tonight?"

"Not at all," he replied nonchalantly.

"You are too," she said in disbelief. "Look at you—you're so uptight, if you farted only dogs would hear it."

The crowd roared at her base humor, which only caused Derek more grief.

Morgan turned to address her audience. "I didn't have time to prepare a speech," she said sweetly, "but I did manage to find a lovely card that perfectly expresses my feelings." She whipped out a small card from her ample bosom, prompting several whistles and catcalls. She cleared her throat and with great dignity read the card aloud:

"You're not old when you need dentures to eat.
You're not old when you trip over your feet.

You're not old when your hair turns gray.
You're not old when you can't remember your name.
You're not old when you can't get to sleep.
You're old when your mind makes a point
That your body can't keep."

Morgan's head drooped to the side when she delivered the last verse, and a thunderous roar of laughter filled the room. "I guess it's true," she added, holding up the card, "Hallmark does make a card for all occasions."

Derek sat frozen, seething in humiliation as he looked around the room at the hundreds of people laughing, but he mustered up the courage to put on a good act.

He stood and gave Morgan an air kiss on each cheek, smiling as though he thought it was funny too, then hugged her tight. "You dried-up hag!" he whispered in her ear through a clenched smile.

Morgan squeezed him as tight as she could, hoping to asphyxiate him. "That's for having me written off the show, you egomaniacal son of a bitch!" she whispered back.

"I'll get you for this!" he threatened as he extricated himself from the bear hug.

Morgan patted him firmly on the back. "Give it your best shot, Gumby," she said with a wink before strutting offstage through the adoring crowd.

Chapter Thirteen

"This is your last chance, buddy," Bailey warned.

"I swear, she's much more your type," Peter said, pleading his case. "She's one of New York's finest...her name's Stella Romano...she's from *Joisey,*" he said, giving it his best New Jersey twang, "but now she lives here in New York. Good Italian stock. She's your height, so that should make you happy, and she works out, so she's got a fit body—although she doesn't have the rack Cheyenne does."

From all the way across the living room, Bailey and Peter became blinded by the light from Alec's grin, which showed every one of his pearly white teeth. "You closet hetero!" Peter shouted to his lover. "Stop that! I thought you were going to watch TV instead of eavesdropping!"

Alec pulled out his trusty *TV Guide* and scanned it, page after page. "*Engraving on the Back Scratcher?*" he grumbled.

Peter looked over at Bailey, indicating she should feel free to take a stab at it. She shook her head, indicating she didn't have a clue. Peter speed walked over to Alec's easy chair and picked up the guide. "*Invasion of the Body Snatchers!*" he groused. "Put yer glasses on!"

Back at the dining table, he sat and shook his head. "My own Mr. Magoo."

The picture Peter found among his photo albums was a pretty good one of Stella at a picnic in Central Park. Bailey liked the well-developed muscles in her arms. "What's her story?" Bailey asked.

"She has no kids and doesn't want to have any. She's very disciplined, obviously, and she's been on the force 11 years. She and her lady friend broke up about two months ago, and she's just started going out again."

"Age?"

"Thirty-four."

Bailey didn't mind a slightly younger woman. After a moment she said, "All right, but I'm telling you—this is it, Peter. This is the last time."

༆

Stella Romano was a darkly attractive woman with ultrashort black hair that she wore combed straight back—and on her, the hairstyle worked. The pants of her black denim suit were snug and showed off her well-developed thigh muscles; the top had a shirttail hem, which she wore out. Bailey assumed that was to hide her lack of a waistline, because that was one of her own fashion techniques.

Bailey and Stella were seated at the Oyster Bar at the Plaza Hotel, and the evening began with one of those painful, awkward pauses. Bailey picked up her menu, figuring they could at least talk about what dishes looked good and what they wanted to order. "Do you want to share a shrimp sampler as an appetizer?" she suggested. "It comes with four kinds of shrimp."

"No, ma'am," Stella said with a cold efficiency in her heavy Jersey twang, as if taking a call from a concerned citizen. "If I have shellfish, my eyes puff up like Rocky in the 14th round." Her head fell back and to one side, arms dangling at her sides. "Cut me, Mick—cut me!" she grunted loudly, imitating Rocky's weak, raspy voice.

Bailey slowly raised the menu to cover her red face. "So...where in Jersey are you from?" she said, her voice muffled slightly by the menu.

"A little town called Deal," Stella replied. Bailey said she'd never heard of it. "It's close to Asbury Park. Springsteen's wife grew up there, I heard. Bunch of filthy rich Syrian Jews, mostly. Just think of Beverly Hills...three-story mansions on two-acre landscaped lots—you get the picture."

"So your parents were well-off, I gather?"

"Oh, no," she said modestly, "my family was there to balance out the economic standard of the community." She sounded like a civil servant issuing a government report. "But one summer I baby-sat for a rich family, and it was like a dream world. I remember going into the kitchen once for a snack and there was this bowl of fresh fruit on the table, only someone hadn't taken the price tags off them. A dollar for each apple!" she said in amazement. "I don't know where them people got their produce, but it wasn't at Ralph's 'cause we were gettin' *our* apples six pounds for a dollar back then.

"They were unbelievable, these fruits," she said, staring at the invisible apple she held in her hands. "I mean *perfect*—not a blemish, perfect color all around, perfectly ripe inside, full of flavor and juice. Unbelievable." She substituted a bread stick for the nonexistent apple and chomped on it. "So what about you?" she said, brushing the crumbs from her black top. "Peter says you got a degree from Harvard? Your family must be doin' all right, then, huh?"

"Not exceptionally...I was lucky enough to get a partial scholarship for my graduate studies at Harvard, but I paid for the rest with my savings."

During another lull, Bailey put down her menu and looked around the restaurant; she noticed three men sitting four tables away, because one of them was giving her a strange look. Oh, well, it wasn't the first time some macho stud got bent out of shape from seeing two women out on a date in public. Get used to it, fella.

After they ordered, to combat the silence, Bailey dug into her bag of first-date questions. "So, it must really be interesting being a police officer in New York City," she said.

"Interesting don't come close. You wouldn't *believe* some of the tales I could tell."

"I'm game," Bailey said, leaning forward.

Stella thought for a moment. "Well...OK...this was, like, a couple of years ago when I was on patrol, before I went to vice. Me and my partner get this call one Sunday morning about a disturbance at a cemetery."

Bailey chuckled. "What was it, some *Night of the Living Dead* scenario?" she said in jest.

"Pretty much."

Bailey's smile evaporated. She regretted initiating this conversation already.

"Seems this family had just buried one of their uncles earlier that week and they were coming out after church to pay their respects and bring fresh flowers—you know the routine.

"Anyway, this particular uncle had been the overweight type, to the tune of about 650 pounds, so the funeral home charged the family $20,000 for a specially made casket. Anyway, these funeral home guys got greedy and decided that if they put the dearly departed in the ground in something cheaper, no one would be the wiser. So they buried the guy in a septic tank and pocketed around fifteen grand—those septic tanks are made to go underground anyway, so it seemed like the perfect scheme, right? Wrong.

"As it happened, it had rained real heavy the night before the family came out, and these morticians— who obviously weren't in the plumbers union—didn't seal the cap properly, and all this rain goes seeping into the tank and turns the dearly departed into a floater. Well, the next day when the grieving family comes to pay their respects, there's Uncle Jack with his hand sticking out of the wet ground waving '*Hullo!*'" she said in a goofy voice waving a hand of her own.

"So the widow keels over from the shock, and the poor groundskeeper, who was the only employee on duty on Sunday, gets surrounded by all these family members about to kill the poor bastard, and he's screaming bloody murder, and someone calls the cops." Stella laughed at the fond remembrance. "That was a good one."

Bailey glanced about to see if anyone else had heard the grotesque account—indeed, the people seated at the neighboring table were scowling at her.

The waiter arrived with their food, and while he was placing the dishes on the table, Bailey noticed the same man a few tables away staring at her again. Get a grip, buddy! Jesus.

She hoped Stella would stop after that appetizing little tidbit, but Officer Romano moved right on to the main course: about an incident that happened after she transferred to the Manhattan vice squad a couple of years ago.

"So I'm doing this undercover sting on this porno shop in midtown that some upper west side dame called in to say was a front for male prostitution."

Her story was interrupted by a loud clatter when their waiter lost his grip on a tray of dishes after catching a whiff of the women's conversation upon his departure. The hostess was in the process of escorting a couple up the same aisle, and the three were now blocked in by the waiter and the mess. Officer Romano automatically went into cop mode and hopped up. "Okay, there's nothing to see here, folks," she said efficiently, as though directing traffic at a highway accident. Then she spoke to the hostess and her customers. "Quit gawking and move it along," she said firmly as she waved them through the row of tables behind her.

Bailey quickly took her napkin from her lap and wiped her mouth, then hid behind the linen veil until Stella returned to the table.

"Anyway," she said, picking up right where she'd left off, "my partner's in one of the private booths in the back of the shop, and before long he sees this little Nazi pecker pokin' through the wall, ready to be sucked or whatever. I said, '*What*—did it have a swastika tattooed on it or something?' and he says, 'No, it was wearing one of those little German helmets—you know, like Sgt. Schultz on *Hogan's Heroes*.'" She laughed heartily. "Dis guy was a *stitch*!" she said, her accent coming out in full force. "God, I miss working with him."

The knot in Bailey's stomach told her she was doomed to never finish a meal at a restaurant again.

"What's wrong?" Stella said, reading the pained look on Bailey's face.

Bailey let out a disgusted puff. "Some guy over there has been staring at me *all night,* and it's really starting to bug me."

Stella looked over her shoulder, and sure enough the guy was still staring. "Jesus, they act like they never seen a dyke before in this city. Rude fuckers." She took a mouthful of coleslaw. "Somehow it still bothers me when that happens, like I'm some kind of freak show. You never quite get used to it, do you?"

There was a certain sadness in Stella's voice that made Bailey feel for her. And of course, she knew exactly what the woman was talking about. Then she saw the man and his two friends heading in her direction on their way to the exit. When they got to her table, the trio stopped. "Excuse me, but have we met before?" the one said to Bailey in a polite manner.

"I don't think so," she said, preparing for his smart-ass reply. She took a sip of wine to wash away the discomfort.

His eyes narrowed. "You know, for some reason you look familiar—something about your eyes and your smile." He reached a little farther back into his memory. "Is your name, by any chance, Mona?"

Suddenly Bailey choked hard on her wine, causing the beverage to dribble all over her white shirt and her good suit. Instantly Stella shrieked, "*Heimlich!*" and sprang to her feet. "*Clear!*" she shouted at the three men blocking her way, then pushed them aside and ran around to the other side of the table, where she grabbed Bailey around her waist. "I'm a trained professional!" she announced, but the victim took her by the hands and stopped her.

In between coughs Bailey mouthed, "It's all right— I'm fine now," she said, quickly guiding Stella back around to her side of the table. "My wine just went down the wrong way."

Soon Bailey regained her composure. Wonderful. This was all she needed, to be busted on a blind date, *by* her date, on a pornography rap. When she recovered enough to speak, she sat back down and said to the man, "No, my name isn't Mona."

"Are you sure?" he said with a little grin, as if trying to coax a yes out of her.

"Hey—Columbo!" Stella snapped. "The lady said it

ain't her name, and I can vouch for that, so take a hike!" she said, pointing to the exit with a thumb over her shoulder.

"Sorry," he said to Bailey, feeling a little embarrassed because half the restaurant was now looking at them. "For some reason that name popped into my head when I saw you. My mistake," he said apologetically, then left with his friends.

Bailey was still reeling from nearly being busted by this jerk when she noticed the stains on her good white dress shirt and suit. At least it was white wine, so it only looked like she'd been pissed on.

❧

As the evening wore on, Bailey discovered Stella enjoyed alcohol just a bit too much for someone with a job requiring so much responsibility. Bailey had drunk only one glass from each of the two bottles of wine they ordered—the rest went into Stella—so by the end of the meal, she was slurring her words and having trouble keeping her heavy eyelids propped open. Bailey figured this was her way of dealing with the stress of the job. She only hoped this one wasn't a horny drunk who would be pawing all over her when she escorted her home.

"Excuse me," Stella said after draining the last drop of wine, "you are paying for dinner, aren't you?"

"Yes."

"Good, 'cause the pants in this pantsuit got no pockets—no place to put a wallet. Can you imagine how impractical that is? Designers just *assume* all women carry purses. I haven't carried a purse since grade school. Anyway, I figured since you did the asking, you'd do the paying too."

"I intended to pay for dinner, yes," Bailey assured her.

"Good. Then I'll stop worrying," she slurred.

Stella suggested taking a walk around Central Park, so the two crossed the street to where the horse-drawn carriages were lined up for the tourists. Stella petted one of them, mumbling her condolences to the animal for having to be enslaved in such a manner.

About halfway down 59th Street, as Bailey was talking about what it was like working for a television network, a good-size rat crawled out from a sewer grate. Bailey wasn't alarmed, because in New York this was an everyday occurrence, but the vermin startled Stella, and instinctively Quick Draw McGraw whipped out her service revolver from the waistband of her pants and blew the furry critter to kingdom come. Everyone on the street went into a panic and began screaming and running for cover behind parked cars and trees. Someone shouted, "Call 911! Call 911!"

Bailey had taken a couple of strides before she realized it was her date who had popped the cap. As Stella replaced the weapon, Bailey understood why the woman left her shirt untucked—to hide her gun. She grabbed Stella by the arm and hustled her down to the corner and across the street, wanting to get as far away from the park as possible.

As they turned down Fourth Street heading south,

Bailey desperately tried to hail a cab—to flee the scene of the crime and get this woman home—but instead, two police cars came wailing up behind them with lights flashing. After coming to a screeching halt, all four officers took cover behind their open car doors and pointed their guns at the women. "*Freeze!*" came the directive.

Bailey stood perfectly still and put her hands up in the air, but Stella wobbled her way to the edge of the sidewalk. "Oh, cut it out, will ya," she said, as if they were playing a game, "I'm a cop!"

"Sure you are, toots!" one of them said. "Why don't you just whip out your badge, then?"

Stella's head zipped back and forth in a negative gesture. "It's at home."

"Yeah—right," another replied, as the two from the front car began circling around to get behind Stella. One leapt forward and grabbed her right hand, jerking it behind her. Then he corralled her left arm and held her securely while his partner frisked her and the back-up cops moved in for reinforcement. "Well, what have we here?" the one said upon removing the revolver from underneath Stella's shirt. He took a quick sniff of the barrel. "Fresh gunpowder," he announced.

The one holding her arms took out his handcuffs and wrestled with the strong woman, trying to get them on her. "So, what were you shooting at?" said the one now holding the gun.

"A rat," she spouted.

"Who? Your ex-boyfriend?" the same officer said.

Stella glared at him. "Do I look like I have a

*boy*friend? Fuckin' moron," she muttered, a little too loudly.

The one with the gun suddenly took the cuffs away from the officer holding her wrists and slapped them on, pinching them together good and tight. "Ow!" Stella cried as she was being led to the patrol car. "You want to loosen these up a little, Officer Krupky?"

"Get in the car and shut up!" he said, shoving her in.

When one of the officers headed toward Bailey, she quickly said, "She really is a police officer. Don't you recognize her?"

"Sure, lady," he said, giving her a quick frisk, "we memorize *every* face on the New York City Police Department...it's part of the test," he spat sarcastically as he dragged Bailey off to the patrol car too, pushing her head down as he shoved her into the back seat next to her date, who was cursing like a sailor.

≥●

The holding tank at the jail was everything the movies had painted it as—and more. It reeked of sour urine—which, of course, you couldn't smell in the movies—because of the toilet standing out in the open in one corner. The floors and benches were filthy, and the skanks they shared the space with didn't smell any better.

There was something so wrong with this picture. Bailey didn't belong here. Hell, she was a *television writer,* for God's sake; even though some people considered that criminal, it really wasn't.

When it came time for her one phone call, she called Peter. After the initial shock, he asked if he needed to bring bail money, but Bailey didn't know. She didn't know whether she was under arrest or being charged or what—this was all new to her and no one had explained what was going on. So Peter said he'd bring cash and a credit card with him, just to be safe. He could tell Bailey was scared and said he'd hurry.

Back in the cell, Bailey asked Stella, "Am I really under arrest? I thought they couldn't do that until after they checked things out on the computer to see if I had a record so they'd have probable cause or whatever?"

"Honey, they can *arrest* anyone they want—they're the police."

Bailey panicked. "So does this mean I'm going to have a record? Oh, God."

Stella patted her on the arm. "If they run a check and you're clean, you won't be *charged,* so you won't have a record. Chill out, sweetie. You'll be fine once they figure out who I am."

It took about half an hour for the desk to get a call back from Stella's precinct officer, who vouched for her. After they were released from the cell, Stella and the goons who arrested her went off in a corner and started talking shop, leaving Bailey standing around growing agitated, wanting to get the hell out of there so she could go home and take a shower.

When she finally lost her patience and walked over to jog her date's memory, Stella offered to have one of the guys give Bailey a ride home in his patrol car, but she declined because Peter was already on his way. She said good night, officially signaling the end to their date.

As Bailey approached the exit, she saw Peter at the information desk and called to him. He held up both hands in defeat and said, "I don't know what happened to you tonight, but you win—I'm throwing in the towel. I will *never* fix you up with anyone again, I swear!" he said, crossing his heart.

"Thank you!" she replied angrily. "I'm going to hold you to that promise," she said, and stormed out the door.

Chapter Fourteen

At 9:47 P.M. that same night, 12 members of the FBI SWAT team were dispatched to a two-story white colonial mansion in the west end of Scarsdale. Three late-model Mercedes, a Lincoln Town Car, and a Cadillac Catera were parked in the driveway. This quiet community of around 15,000 upper-class homes was far from the standard run-down hovel these men usually encountered on a drug bust or a mob racketeering sting.

From behind a tall, sculpted boxwood shrub next to the front door, Harry Mulvane nudged his partner, Jason Crossfield, as they waited for the six members assigned to the upstairs portion of the house to get themselves positioned in trees and on the roof. "Jesus Christ," Mulvane groused in his thick Bronx accent, "whaddya think houses go for in this neighborhood?"

"Let's see...6,000 square feet...two-acre lot...mmm,

about five mill." Crossfield made his assessment with all the assurance of a real estate agent.

Mulvane shook his head enviously. "Hard to think some loon has the loot to buy a joint like this—this is as big as a friggin' grocery store."

Crossfield appraised the front exterior of the house. "Look at that nice leaded-glass double door."

"Yeah," his partner sighed, thinking it made a sweet sight, "two swans with their necks sorta making a heart."

"Too bad we're gonna have break their pretty little necks," Crossfield said sadly, just seconds before the team commander gave the signal that sent the 12 men in black, all brandishing automatic assault rifles, busting in through the front and back doors and several windows from all sides of the house.

After treading through a sea of shattered glass, the agents dashed from room to room, upstairs and down, heavy footsteps pounding through the well-furnished home, searching for its occupants. But they found no one. "I know they're here," the commander said with frustration, "we got the word from the surveillance team less than an hour ago that they definitely saw movement from inside the house."

"You don't think they sent us to the wrong house, do you? It's happened before," one said.

"God, I hope not," the commander said, then turned, preparing to go through the house one more time, until he noticed a door partially hidden under the stairwell—a basement. He smiled.

He pointed at the door, then held up eight fingers,

meaning he wanted eight men rushing in, leaving four to secure the rest of the house. Quietly, he turned the knob on the door.

Mulvane led the charge down the stairs shouting, "FBI! Stay where you are!" A shriek of high-pitched voices hung in the air. When the commander entered, he couldn't believe his eyes.

In the middle of the huge underground recreation room, five gray-haired ladies stood with their hands in the air, each shaking like Chihuahuas. The huge room had been converted into a print shop and assembly line, complete with a computer and printer, stacks of envelopes, reams of paper, and rolls of stamps. A pile of folded, printed letters was ready to be stuffed into the pile of waiting envelopes beside it. The walls were covered with pictures of Morgan Gable and many of the other stars of *All the Bold Days of My Restless Life*.

"Please don't hurt us!" cried 80-year-old Maude Keller in a frail, quavering voice. "I never keep cash in the house, but take our purses—they're over there on the coffee table," she said, pointing a trembling finger.

"No, ma'am, we're from the FBI," the commander stated.

"The FBI? The *real* FBI?" said 68-year-old Bertha Cox, seeming quite impressed with their destructive visitors.

"Ladies, we tracked you down through your letters to NBS threatening the show's writers. Do you realize it's a federal offense to make death threats through the mail?"

All five gray-haired women looked thoroughly confused. "Death threats?"

≥▲

Maude and her four cohorts sat in Mike Mahoney's office the following day explaining to the producer what they had done, with Bailey and an Agent Drummond from the FBI also in attendance. "So you see, we weren't threatening to kill anyone—we were just trying to say, quite boldly, that if the show didn't keep Binaca Blaylock on, we would stop watching. We didn't mean we'd kill anyone—my heavens!"

Bertha sat forward. "All our children have grown up and now have families and lives of their own—they've practically deserted us," she said sadly. "These characters in Fairview are the only lives we have to get involved with anymore. Maybe we did sound a bit too strong in our letters without realizing it. If we did, we're genuinely sorry, Mr. Mahoney."

"We thought we were being rather clever, sending the black flowers," Enid Boreland boasted. "It seemed so much more effective than just saying we would stop watching the show."

Mike had to laugh at that one. "Well, you were right there. It certainly did have an effect," he said, glancing toward Agent Drummond.

"So what's going to happen to us?" Maude timidly inquired.

"Are you going to send us to the slammer?" Eugenie Flowers croaked.

"I can't do hard time," Velma Lyndon said forcefully, patting the aluminum apparatus in front of her. "I have to use a walker...and you know what happens to the weak and injured in prison," she said, nearly in tears. "They get culled from the herd." Velma grew horrified at the thought of what awaited her in the Big House as Maude, who was sitting beside her, put a comforting arm around her shoulders.

Mike and Agent Drummond had to stifle a laugh at the image of these little old ladies in the middle of a prison-yard rumble. Mike stood and addressed the ladies. "I'll talk to the network heads this afternoon and explain everything to them. I'm certain they won't want to press charges since this has turned out to be just a big misunderstanding and no real harm was done."

The ladies exhaled in relief, and each apologized copiously on their way out as they shook hands with Mike Mahoney then with Agent Drummond, who departed with them.

"So," Bailey said to Mike, "do you think Stubblefield will back off?"

"He has to. They can't press charges against five widowed grandmothers—how would that look in the press?"

Bailey sighed. Ah yes, image...that was the network's main concern. But this time she had to agree with them—if they pursued little old ladies, they'd really get hate mail—and she chuckled at the whole scenario. "That was pretty clever, sending those black flowers," she said. Then something occurred to her. "Hey, what do you say we give those ladies each a free ticket to the live show? I'll bet they'd love it, since they're such fans. You know—a little good-will gesture."

Mike beamed. "That's a great idea, Bailey. I'll make sure it's taken care of," he said.

Bailey sat back, feeling relieved that it was all over, and decided it must be a good omen for the final show.

੨੭

Two days before the live show, the cast and crew all congregated at Radio City Music Hall for the first rehearsal. Because the regular daily schedule also had to be conducted, this rehearsal had to take place in the evening, after everyone had gotten a dinner break and a few hours to unwind.

Myriad sets were still half-decorated, and the smell of fresh wood and paint hung heavy in the atmosphere, despite the half-dozen giant fans whirring furiously in an effort to suck the toxic fumes stage right and blow them outside through several sets of open doors.

Blaine took charge of the group, a script in each hand. "Okay, folks," he shouted to be heard over the sawing and hammering and whirring, "this show is basically the same format as our everyday taping, with four 11-minute segments, each followed by a four-minute commercial break. Only this time, those four minutes are going to be filled with a dozen stagehands furiously changing sets, so stay out of their way—is that clear?"

A grumbling of acknowledgment arose.

"And because this is Morgan's farewell performance, we've got her wedding as the main story line, with the Aruba-Beau-Pashmina triangle as our only subplot—

after all, it's Binaca's wedding people will be tuning in to see. So, the rest of you—which I'm sure you noticed when you read the script—have been woven into these scenes in supporting roles so that everyone is included in this historic live show."

He clasped his hands and rubbed them together vigorously. "So, we start with Beau's speech to Pashmina, where he's trying to decide what to do about the baby, et cetera, et cetera. Beau and Pashmina—hit your marks, please. Aruba, stand by. The rest of you, quiet please."

Mitch and the actress who played Pashmina took their proper places on the huge stage and began the scene, which took place at Beau's house.

The couple went error-free through the entire dramatic dialogue, which ended with Pashmina throwing a glass of wine in his face and rushing out of the house in tears.

"All right," Blaine said, "Beau goes to his bedroom and takes off his wet polo shirt and jeans, preparing to take a shower to wash up from the wine." After giving Mitch sufficient time to go through the motions, he said, "Then he gets out his suitcases preparing to pack. Cue Aruba!"

Heather entered the stage and stomped three times on the wooden floor in lieu of knocking on a door that wasn't built yet, while Blaine continued the narration. "When Beau opens the door in nothing but his muscles and bikini briefs, Aruba gives him the once-over and says—" He pointed to Heather.

"Well, don't you look buffed and beautiful

tonight...you must have sensed I was coming...or would be soon, perhaps," she purred with a wicked smile as she barged her way in, rubbing up against Beau's front in a sexual manner as she passed. Soon she turned to where the bedroom would be and look shocked. "Are you going somewhere?" she asked.

"I'm leaving to sort things out, Aruba," Beau said, wringing his hands. "I was all set to marry Pashmina, but now that you're pregnant with my baby—I have to go and figure out what's the right thing to do."

Aruba turned frantically and gasped in despair. "But, where are you going? Are you going back home to stay with your family?"

"No, I can't go back there—ever," he said, arousing her suspicions.

"Why not?"

After wrestling with his conscience, he finally comes clean. "Because I have an outstanding arrest warrant for something I did when I was younger...something b-a-a-a-d." He turned away in anguish, biting the back of his hand. Mitch tried to sound wicked, but he hadn't been hired because of his acting ability, and the scene looked almost comical to Bailey and Peter, who were camped out in the wings watching on a closed-circuit TV.

"You know how they say you can never go home again? Well, that's me. I can never go back to Clarksville. If I do, they'll all be waiting for me."

"Who? Who will be waiting for you, Beau?"

"The authorities...along with all the people whose lives I ruined!" He made a dramatic turn toward the imaginary camera for his close-up. "All those poor people!" He bit his hand again.

"Hold for music," Blaine instructed as he checked the stopwatch in his hand, "a-a-a-nd we're out!" he said, punching the button atop the watch to stop it. "Great job, folks. Nice level of drama." The three actors got a congratulatory pat on the back from the director for a job well done, then all those in the wedding rehearsal dinner scene were given their call.

"Okay, we're at the country club seated at several large, round tables," he said, pointing to the cheap metal folding chairs that had been placed in circles around nothing on the center set, "except those in the wedding party, who obviously are seated at the long table at the front of the room," he added, then pointed to the line of chairs at the back of the stage. "We open with dinner being served."

As people took their places, another cloud of toxic fumes floated in—one that was strong enough to overpower the paint and varnish. It was coming from Derek, who left a vapor trail from a three-pitcher martini dinner as he breezed in. "Well," Morgan sneered as she took her seat, "if it isn't the eighth dwarf, Droopy."

Several of the cast wondered to themselves what she meant by that; Derek stopped short for a microsecond, then pretended the remark was just a general insult from his nemesis and plopped down in the chair beside her just as the waiter approached the bridal couple. "Will you be having the beef or lobster?" he said to the groom.

"The lovely lady will have the beef Wellington," Ace

said, squeezing Binaca's hand affectionately, "and I shall have the lobster thermidor."

After dinner, the best man made several toasts to the happy couple, and as with tradition, the toast turned into a roast of the bride and groom.

Zirconia Deardorf, the matron of honor and college chum of Binaca, stood to take her turn. "You two have known each other only a short time, and I'm guessing the groom doesn't know everything in Binaca's closets." The intrigued guests grew all atwitter.

"Ace, I'll bet you had no idea that your bride-to-be was once a Las Vegas showgirl!" Zirconia said, causing everyone to gasp with shock and surprise. "For about two hours," she explained with a laugh. "It was the summer after our freshman year at Smith, and she'd gotten a summer job at one of the big hotels through her uncle, who just happened to own the hotel," she said in a way that emphasized the nepotism involved, "but it seems the headdress she had to wear her first night was too heavy for little Binaca, and she kept falling over! She got demoted to waitress that same night!" Everyone applauded and had a good laugh at the blushing bride. "And that's the real woman you're marrying tomorrow," she said, then walked over and gave Binaca a kiss on the cheek before returning to her chair.

"Now, the orchestra will play 'Blue Moon,' and everyone takes to the dance floor," Blaine said. "Ace and Binaca are up front here, cuddling and cooing for the camera."

The couple approached the front of the stage and

began slow dancing. "Binaca, my dear, your past doesn't matter a whit to me," Ace said sweetly. "I find it quite noble that even though you come from a wealthy family, you found such an industrious way to put yourself through college. Yes, I know being a showgirl isn't the most dignified profession, but you were young then—this was something that happened a long time ago. It just means we're going to have something to look back on fondly as we grow old together," he said, then looked deeply into her eyes and kissed her on the cheek. He held the kiss until Blaine called the scene.

"Okay, the third segment switches between the dressing rooms at the church, with Ace and Binaca each expressing their feelings about this special day that is finally upon them as they get dressed."

The action moved to the third set, where everyone took their places and began at a quick pace.

"Okay," Blaine said, as they came to the dramatic part, "at the end of the scene, Binaca comes out and stands by a leaded-glass window to check her makeup, looking radiant. Zirconia admires the bride and dabs her eye with a handkerchief and says—"

"You look so beautiful standing there...the way the angle of the light hits you just so," Zirconia said.

Derek took a few steps toward the edge of the stage so he could see what was going on over on the other half of the set with the womenfolk. "What kind of geometry is she using?" he blurted out with a snarl.

Blaine quickly got Derek under control again, and the scene finished without a hitch. Then they moved on to the final segment, the wedding itself.

"Now, at the beginning of the final segment, Binaca will make her grand entrance from the top of the staircase on the right side of the house and come onstage to organ music from the Mighty Wurlitzer beneath the stage, which of course will be played by Elton Johnson, the organist at Fairview Methodist Church."

"Where is he?" Heather asked.

"He's not here today," Mike explained. "They can't get the organ to come up, so we'll have to wait until tomorrow for the music."

His choice of words prompted Morgan to grin. "Can't get the old organ up, huh?" she taunted within earshot of Derek. "What a pity." Derek glared at Morgan, then hurried over to his mark.

Morty grew concerned about what he had just heard about the staging of this scene. "Blaine, you realize that the back of this staircase is about 160 feet from the stage...you'd better make sure your organist doesn't have arthritis."

Blaine took into consideration Morty's concern and instructed Morgan to make a swift but graceful approach during the bridal march.

Noting the concern on many faces about all the kinks that still needed to be worked out in less than 48 hours, Blaine—uncharacteristically—decided to offer some words of encouragement. "At least we've got the most important set finished," Blaine said, admiring the dual set at the right side of the stage, which comprised the church and the bell tower. "All right—quiet, and let's begin the ceremony."

The preacher took his mark, ready to preside.

"Dearly beloved," he said, "we are gathered here today in the presence of God and all these witnesses to join together Chauncey 'Ace' Atkinson and Binaca Blaylock in the bonds of holy matrimony. It is not a union to be entered into lightly..."

Soon he instructed Ace to repeat after him, and the actor obliged.

At the end of the vows, the preacher said to the groom, "Do you take this woman to be your lawfully wedded wife, to have and to hold, for better or for worse, in sickness and in health, till death do you part?"

Derek held his head high and said, "I'd like to answer that as Jim Carrey would," then he bent over and took hold of his butt cheeks and said, "I d-o-o-o!" but the last word was muffled by a loud, rippling fart.

Blaine motioned for the confused reverend to continue with the vows, and Ace then slipped the ring onto Binaca's finger.

The bride repeated her vows until Blaine interrupted with more direction. "Okay, when Binaca says the 'till death do us part' line, Camera 3 comes in close, and we pause for dramatic effect, because something is stirring inside her—some hidden torment—some deep anguish." Binaca exhibited the appropriate facial expression, and the scene continued.

"With this ring, I thee wed," she said, and pretended to place the golden band on Ace's finger.

The preacher closed his Bible and smiled. "I now pronounce you man and—"

"*Stop!*" Binaca shouted, "I can't go through with this!"

Blaine went into action again. "Okay, this is where all the guests and extras in the congregation gasp with shock." All the actors looked around. "What extras?" one of them asked, seeing only the regular cast in attendance.

Blaine waved it off. "A screwup in casting—we'll have about 20 extras at the rehearsal dinner scene and 20 more at the church during the wedding on Friday."

"They're not coming to any of the rehearsals?" Heather said in shock.

"Don't worry about it," Blaine said confidently, "how much instruction do people need to sit and watch? Now, Binaca—finish your line and rush out."

"I can't do this to you, my love—" Morgan seemed to have the words of her next line sticking to her tongue. "My love," she repeated, then smacked her lips, making an awful face. "Kinda leaves a bad taste in your mouth," she said, but quickly got back into character and continued. "I can't marry you!" she cried in anguish.

Blaine hopped up. "Now, Binaca runs off, down the aisle and through the archway over to the other half of the set to the bell tower," he said, "and Ace follows." He waved Derek over to his mark.

"Okay, cue Binaca!"

"I have something to confess to you, Ace," Binaca said in tears. "I know everyone in Fairview thinks I inherited my money from my father, but that's not true. You see...I was married before."

"No shit!" Derek said, referring to her real marriage record.

"Derek!" Blaine shouted. "Can we just get through this final scene without going off-script, please?"

Morgan collected herself. "And I got almost $10 million from his life insurance when he died," she said dramatically.

Ace walked over and took her by the shoulders. "That's nothing to be ashamed of, my dear."

"But what you don't know is, my husband died of liver failure...which I induced by injecting him with concentrated vitamin A."

Ace looked uncertain. "I don't believe you."

"It's true!" she cried, breaking away. "I hated him—I wanted out of the marriage, but he wouldn't let me have a divorce," she said, pacing frantically, wringing her hands. "He used to beat me every time I tried to leave. Finally I snapped, and one night I killed him!" She turned to Ace and took him by the hand. "So you see, that's why I can't marry you...I couldn't bear to ruin your reputation and turn you into a social outcast in your own hometown because you're married to a murderer!"

Derek clasped her hands in his. "But you had justification," he said with assurance. "And I promise you I'll never tell anyone. Should the authorities ever get suspicious, we'll get you the best attorney money can buy. No jury in their right mind would convict you after hearing all this."

"No!" she cried. "I can't. I murdered my husband, and I must be punished for it!" Binaca broke away, ran to the balustrade surrounding the bell tower, and stepped up onto the top railing.

"Binaca!" Ace shouted, lurching toward her, then stopping for fear of scaring her over the edge.

"Okay, Morgan," Blaine said, "make sure the air mattress is in the right spot for you."

Morgan looked down at the rotund stagehand in overalls about 10 feet beneath her who was in charge of the stunt mattress. "To the left a little," she instructed. "Okay, that's fine."

"Then, bon voyage!" Blaine shouted, giving her a salute.

Morgan turned to Derek, getting back into character. "Goodbye, Ace, my darling." But she couldn't muster the courage to jump.

After about 15 seconds Derek said, "Where are my manners?" and he took a step toward Morgan with arms outstretched. "Let me help you," he said with great zeal.

Morgan clutched one of the pillars rising from the railing to the roof of the tower. "Keep away from me, putzboy!" she shouted. "I'll jump when I'm ready!" The actress took in a deep breath and closed her eyes. "Goodbye, Ace, my darling—*a-a-a-h!*"

As she disappeared over the balustrade, Ace cried, "No, Binaca—*n-o-o-o!*" and rushed frantically to the railing. Immediately he turned away, shielding his eyes from the horrifying sight below. "I can't bear to look, to see the woman I love this way." He slumped to the floor, clutching his heart. "Oh, God, if only she could come back for just a few seconds...so I could tell her one last time how much I love her.

"She was such a delicate creature...she was always so beautiful no matter what she wore." He pulled

out a handkerchief and dabbed his eyes as he delivered a few more lines.

"For me, she'll never really be gone...I'll always have
that last, lingering image of her today in her beautiful
bridal gown."

"And we're out!" Blaine cried. "That was great," the
director said insincerely while he checked his watch,
"and we're only 17 minutes over schedule." General
grousing erupted. "All right—tomorrow night, dress
rehearsal from start to finish, no stops for anything and
no straying from the script," he said, glaring at Derek.
"Six o'clock sharp, folks. Makeup, hair, and costumes
here at the music hall, not at the studio!" He shook his
head and grumbled to Marci, "Someone will forget."

"Undoubtedly," she replied.

੪

That evening Derek sat in his Sutton Place apartment, sipping on a brandy in front of the fireplace,
listening to a recording of his favorite opera, with
Maria Callas as Tosca. He was angry at Morgan for
her "eighth dwarf" remark, which made him think
about that insidious poem she had read aloud in front
of all his closest friends at his birthday party. How
humiliating. And how many of them must have
laughed and wondered whether it was really just a
joke? Damn that bitch!

And yet, if there had been some way he could have
gotten her into the sack, she might have been the cure
for what ailed him. He would have given anything for

the chance to nail that broad. Too bad he didn't have something on her like she did on him.

He closed his eyes, his thoughts melding with the opera unfolding, and soon he was picturing Maria Callas in the bell tower suicide scene. Aah, if only he could throw Morgan over the edge instead of her jumping. Now, that would be sweet revenge.

Suddenly, through the clouds in his head, a memory came shining through—a memory from his youth long ago, from the first time he had seen *Tosca* at the New York City Opera in the early '60s with his parents.

The revelation filled him with delight. How could he have forgotten something so outrageously diabolical?

Derek sat forward, a spark of evil genius glowing like brimstone in his eyes as his plan for revenge came together in an instant. "Perfect!" he gloated.

Chapter Fifteen

"Where the hell is Mitch?" Blaine yelled, because it was now 6 o'clock and everyone else was in costume and ready to begin the dress rehearsal. "Anybody heard from him?" the angry director inquired, but got no answer. "Well, try his cell phone and his house!" he snapped at Marci, who hopped to it. But without even waiting until she had dialed all the numbers, he yelled, "We're just going to have to read around him." Then he spotted Peter and Bailey in the wings. "Peter! Can you do Beau for us today?"

Peter whispered lecherously to Bailey, "I could do Beau for them any day." Then he said to Blaine, "Sure, be right there!" He picked up his copy of the script, and like a bad ventriloquist spoke out of the corner of his mouth, "Don't leave for the party without me—I don't want to get stuck riding to the restaurant with those vipers." Bailey, who was dressed in her special Armani suit for Morgan's farewell celebration with the cast after rehearsal, gave Peter her assurance that she'd wait for him.

Derek was Mr. Goody Two Shoes and made it through the entire rehearsal dinner scene without any embellishments, which aroused Morgan's suspicions. After the scene was finished, she cocked an eyebrow and said in a heavy Russian accent, "Shouldn't you be out making beeg t-r-r-ouble fo-r-r-r moose and squi-r-r-r-el?"

"I don't know what you mean," he said, sounding genuinely confused.

"What are you up to?" she replied, not buying the act.

His hands went out helplessly. "Nothing. I was just hoping that perhaps you would allow me to escort you to your farewell celebration after rehearsal tonight," he said politely.

Morgan snarled instantly. "In your dreams!" she spat out before storming off in a huff.

Derek stood with his hands in his pockets and smiled as he watched her stomp away.

۶ₐ

Forty minutes into the dress rehearsal, things had been going swimmingly and Bailey was encouraged, until Mike came rushing up and took her aside. "You're going to have to do a quick rewrite," he said urgently.

"On this scene?" she said, meaning the one that was in progress.

"On the whole show."

She let out a laugh of contempt. "Like hell! This thing is gold, baby! I'm not changing a word of it."

"I think you might want to change your mind about that," he said.

"Why?" she asked, looking into his stoic face for a clue.

"Because Mitch Carrington just got fired."

"*What?*" Bailey went apoplectic, seeing her show, her glorious, history-making show, spiraling down the drain. Mike shushed her, because no one else on the show knew yet. "Why?" she asked.

"Because Lindsay Stubblefield is pregnant...and it's his kid."

Bailey couldn't believe her ears. This couldn't be true. "That's absurd! He's been dating some gorgeous brunette since the first of the year, and Lindsay's had her leg in a cast until a month ago. That can't be."

"Yeah, well, you know what a babe hound Mitch is— he was spending time with Lindsay on the side for some reason, and one night the gorgeous brunette comes over to his apartment and finds him boffing the little blond. She dumps him, and whaddya know—little Lindsay ends up with a bun in the oven...and guess who's the baker?" He could see Bailey was overwhelmed with disbelief. "And you didn't even write this one!"

"But the network can't do this to us now—the show is tomorrow—*live!* Don't they know that? It was their idea! Won't they let him stay on at least through tomorrow?"

Mike shook his head. "No way, no how. Stubblefield called Mr. Studmuffin up to his office right after the taping today and told him to get the hell out of town. He had security take him over to the studio and stand over him while he cleared out his dressing room, then escort him to the door, where they took away his security pass. He's history. I heard he's already subleased his apartment and is packed and ready to leave town."

Bailey frantically circled Mike, trying to think. "I don't believe this. Where's he going?"

"To Australia. He's going to work as a chum slinger in his uncle's shark hunting business in Sydney."

Bailey scowled at the disgusting image. From hunk to tossing chunks. Ulghk! "Well, what the hell are we supposed to do? We can't do a rewrite now—in case they haven't looked at a calendar, today is Thursday, and the live show is Friday—tomorrow Friday! We can't change the script—all the sets and props have been ordered according to this one and are already finished, as you can see. This isn't like a taping, Mike, where we have three weeks until air to change things around—it won't work! This is like a Broadway play, there are limitations, and one of those limitations is *no rewrites the day before the show!*" she screamed hysterically.

Mike had never seen Bailey have a complete meltdown before, and he tried to calm her down. "Well...just stick one of the other actors in tomorrow to read Mitch's lines."

"There are no extra actors!" she shrieked, clenching her fists. "This is a historic event for this show, and everyone wanted to be in it, so they are—as their own characters—they've each got lines in at least one scene!" she explained. "Besides, the audience would never fall for that—one of the other characters suddenly becoming Beauregard Buchanan? That's insane!"

An idea hit Mike. "Wait a minute—I got a letter a

couple of weeks ago from that guy who used to play the Chippendale's dancer—oh, what was that character's name?"

"Rock Hard," Bailey replied instantly.

"Yeah—that's the one. I forget his real name, but he's been bouncing around town the last two years trying to get a movie career going, and it sounded like he was fishing to get back on the show."

Bailey recalled the actor. "He was built a lot like Mitch, all buffed and bronzed—for all those Speedo dance scenes."

"He's familiar with the show too—he knows most of the characters."

"Who cares about that—he doesn't know the lines. How the hell is he going to memorize an entire segment in less than 24 hours?"

"We'll use cue cards, just to be safe," he said, looking to Bailey for approval to his idea.

"Well, don't just stand there—give the guy a call, for Christ's sake!"

"I've got his letter at my office with his contact info on it—I'll call you as soon as I locate him," he said, and dashed off.

A sinking feeling gripped Bailey's stomach, and she rubbed her throbbing temples. "This is not good. This is not good."

❧

The dress rehearsal ended only six minutes over schedule, which was close enough for Blaine and Bailey.

Both agreed they were going to forget about the show and enjoy Morgan's celebration.

As the group was filing out of Radio City, someone asked, "Where's Derek?"

"He said he had some last-minute thing to take care of," someone else replied.

ॐ

Behind the bell tower set, the large stagehand in overalls was marking off with masking tape the exact location of the air mattress for Binaca to fall on, when he saw a shadow in the curtains. Derek walked up and put an arm around the startled man in a very cozy fashion. "There's been a slight change in the final scene, my good man," the dignified actor said.

The stagehand looked puzzled. "I wasn't notified of no change," he said.

Derek pulled out five crisp $100 bills from the breast pocket of his blazer and fanned them out in front of the man's face. "Mr. Franklin has just notified you."

He looked both ways and, seeing no witnesses, plucked the bills from Derek's hand and stuffed them into his own pocket. Derek smiled and began explaining exactly what the change was to be.

ॐ

A few blocks away at Le Cirque, which had been reserved especially for Morgan's party, the group had just been served appetizers when Bailey's cell phone rang. It was Mike Mahoney.

"Now?" she said disappointedly, scooping a spoonful of French onion soup into her mouth. "Can't you tell me over the phone—we're right in the middle of our celebration dinner...oh, all right, I'll be there as soon as I can."

She stuffed the phone back into her jacket and shoveled in more soup. "That was Mike," she whispered to Peter, in whom she had confided Mitch's departure. "He was on a hot trail to find a sub for Mitch and I'll bet he crapped out." She scraped the edges and the bottom of the crockery bowl to get every bit, then licked the spoon thoroughly. "Jesus Christ," she said when she realized what was happening, "we're going to end up using a substitute actor to fill in for Mitch on live TV...well, fuck me running!" she groused, tossing the spoon into the empty dish with a loud clink as she stood to leave.

Her choice of words puzzled Peter, and while Bailey bitched and moaned as she gathered her belongings, he dealt with a mental picture, trying to figure out just how that would be possible. He quickly gave up and volunteered to go along with Bailey for moral support.

੨ଈ

Peter had just turned on the TV in Bailey's office and gotten cozy in her executive leather chair when she walked in from her meeting with Mike looking stunned and pale. "Don't tell me," he said sarcastically, "they fired Morgan the day before her big farewell." He didn't expect much from the morons in the ivory tower who had already put them in such a bind.

"No," she said softly, "they fired me."

Peter shot to his feet. "Why are they firing you?"

"Because Lindsay's pregnant."

He paused for a moment. "Uh, Stubblefield doesn't think that you..." He did the wavering hand, wondering whether Lindsay's father thought Bailey might somehow be the one who had done the dirty deed.

"How the hell could I knock the girl up?" Bailey said disgustedly as she approached her desk. "No, Lindsay ran off to Australia with Mitch to sling chum," she groused, "but before she left, she wrote Daddy a note explaining everything, asking him to thank me for giving her that 'special assignment.' So now he blames me for thrusting his baby girl together with that cad who impregnated her.

"He was on the phone with Mike the whole time, and I could hear him shrieking, dictating exactly what to say to me. They've given me two weeks notice," Bailey groaned as she flopped into her chair, looking around at the office that had been her second home for six years, dreading having to pack up all her things.

"Excuse me, but isn't it usually the other way around—you give them two weeks notice?"

"They would have dumped me today, but they don't want to make a big stink and cast a dark shadow over the show right before the Emmys, when all the media are focused on the soaps. They've already issued a press release saying Mitch will be replaced on tomorrow's show due to an 'undisclosed illness.' But having to explain firing their head writer on the same day would open the flood gates of the media."

"Those bastards," Peter said, hands on hips. "Well, isn't that great—you get to stay until you pick up your Emmy, then they'll rip it out of your hands as soon as you get to the wings and give you the network boot up your ass," he said, kicking her desk. "Those ungrateful pricks! After six years with this show, this is how they treat you? You ought to just type up your resignation and not give them the satisfaction!"

"I can't. It's in our contract. It's a one-way option...theirs."

"You're kidding?"

"Read the fine print—it's in everyone's contract."

Peter looked doubtful. "This isn't like the Kidney Clause, is it?" he asked. Bailey shook her head. He sighed helplessly. "You poor baby. Come on—you need a drink."

⁊

The two had schlepped around the block to Pete's Bar & Grill, where Bailey was now leaning on an elbow, staring off into space, well into her first glass of wine. "What's happened to me, Peter?" she lamented. "I used to have the Midas touch...everything I touched turned to gold. Now I've got the toilet touch...everything I touch turns to shit," she proclaimed as she finished off her wine in one gulp.

"What are you going to do now?" he asked.

She shrugged. "Well, I do have an MBA from

Harvard...maybe I'll put it to use and open a restaurant or something."

Peter smiled as though that were the niftiest idea he'd ever heard. "Uh-huh, and just for safekeeping, you might want to take the rest of your life savings and shred it through the garbage disposal!"

Bailey abandoned the restaurant idea, and one glass of wine had turned into two bottles an hour and a half later, when Peter finally stuffed Bailey into a cab and took her home.

❧

The boss was stumbling a bit, so he escorted her up to her apartment, just to make sure she got there safe and sound, and deposited her on the couch while he went out to the kitchen to put on some coffee. Then he used the phone in Bailey's bedroom to call Alec and explain why he'd be a little late getting home.

When Peter got back to the living room, Bailey was halfway through a Scotch on the rocks. "Oh, honey," he said with great concern, "after drinking red wine all night, that good Scotch is going to taste like piss."

"Do not fret, my good man," she slurred, "I cleansed my palate with Cool Ranch Doritos between courses." She poured the leftover chip crumbs into her gaping mouth directly from the bag. "By the way, what are those tiny red droplets on my kitchen floor?" she asked as she sprawled out on the couch, with limp arms at her side, head resting on the back of the couch while she stared through the ceiling.

"Oh, sorry," he said, looking a little embarrassed, "when I was getting the cream for our coffee, I saw the watermelon in there. I can't resist ripe watermelon—you know that."

"Oh...it looks like blood," she said, unfazed. "Scared me for a second."

Peter sat down next to Bailey. "You know, you don't have to worry about anything. You can start another career—you're still young."

"I know," she pined, "I would have been 39 my next birthday," she added, feeling as though she'd never make it to June 22. "I don't know what I'll do, Peter. Maybe I'll go on Broadway...I'll do a one-woman revival of *Cats*," she said, picking up Puddin, who had curled up on her lap. She stepped grandly onto the coffee table, and to the familiar melody of "Memories" she sang, "M-i-i-i-dn-i-i-i-ght, all the kitties are sl-e-e-e-ping."

It was all Peter could do to keep from laughing at the pitiful sight.

"Or maybe something more peppy, like *Fame!* Yeah—I got it," she said, lifting Puddin like a barbell and shouting, "Mange! I wanna shed forever!" to the tune of the famous title song.

Puddin didn't want any more to do with this box-office bomb and pushed off from Bailey's chest, high-tailin' it out of there. When the star stepped down from the stage, her legs went all rubbery, and she duck-walked a few steps before Peter could grab her. "Man!" she huffed with wide eyes, "there is way too much gravity in this room." She managed to get the words out just before she went splatto all over the dining table in front of the windows, where she lay motionless like a beached whale.

When she hadn't moved after a minute, Peter said, "Are you all right?" then he felt her forehead, checking for fever.

"Yeah," she whined pathetically, "I'm just resting up for that big sale at Dykes R Us. Maybe I'll finally be able to find a decent-fitting suit at a decent price...ya think?"

As Peter returned to the couch and poured some cream in his coffee, it finally hit Bailey. This suit! It was this damn suit she was wearing that had cursed her! She had worn it on all three of her disastrous dates, and again today, when she got fired. It was this friggin' $4,000 suit giving her a dose of instant karma for being so vain and extravagant and phony!

Bailey slid off the table and immediately began disrobing, wanting to get out of the garment as soon as possible to halt the curse. Peter, having not been privy to that inner monologue, started to wonder whether his boss had gone totally desperate and was doing this strip tease to entice him.

After shedding her pants and jacket, Bailey picked them up, turning them this way and that like a magician so her audience of one could see there was nothing fishy about the items used in this trick. Then she walked over to the window and pushed it open, held up the suit, and tossed it straight out. For her imaginary audience, she flung her empty hands into the air in a silent ta-d-a-a-a! while bearing a look of amazement and satisfaction that the suit had mysteriously disappeared before their very eyes. Bailey strode away from the window with bouncy steps, wiping any residue of the tainted pantsuit from her hands, then took a bow. Big mistake.

Peter caught her just before she hit the floor. "Girl, I am putting you to bed," he groaned as he struggled with the stocky, limp woman.

Once he had bundled her into his arms, a truly strange feeling came over him, because he was now touching his half-naked boss, who was clad only in a white dress shirt, undies, and white socks. It had worked on Tom Cruise, but not on Bailey.

He managed to lift her securely into his arms and carry her down the hall, his skinny legs bowing with every step because she outweighed him by a good 20 pounds.

Halfway down the hall, Bailey groaned loudly. "Oh, man—I think those Cool Ranch Doritos are gonna cleanse my palate one more time!"

Peter heeded the warning and immediately backed up a couple of steps, veering left into the guest bathroom.

꒰ꔷ꒱

Peter tossed Bailey unceremoniously onto her bed, and she rolled over once so that she was face-up in the middle of the mattress. He straightened the sheet and pulled it up to cover her, and she took him by the hand. "You're a good friend, Peter," she said with eyes closed, "except when you try to fix me up." Then she issued an ominous warning as she wagged a finger. "If you dare try to fix me up again, may the blood of the watermelon be on your head."

He snickered, but not so loud as to insult her. "I promise I'll stop playing matchmaker," he said as he tucked the sheet in around her shoulders. At that moment he noticed a tear roll off her cheek onto the pillow.

"Why is it so hard, Peter?" she sniffled. "Why can't I meet my Alec?" she said, wiping her eyes with the sheet. "You're so lucky."

"I know," he said, touching the ring Alec had given him as a symbol of love and devotion eight years ago. "I guess I'm better at picking out a good man than I am at finding you a good woman."

Bailey patted his hand drunkenly. "You're a good friend. I suppose I should have waited longer after Miranda left—it was just too soon." She sniffled again, then took a deep breath. "Well, from now on I'm concentrating strictly on work...I should say on finding work."

"Don't worry about that now," he said. "We have a big day ahead of us tomorrow...get some sleep."

Chapter Sixteen

"Isn't this fabulous!" Bertha Cox said to her four friends as they gawked at the neon marquee of Radio City Music Hall that stretched between 50th and 51st streets. The ladies had dressed in their Sunday best—complete with hats and white gloves—as had many of the 6,000 guests at today's wedding gala who were filing in.

Once inside the lobby, the women were awestruck by the geometric pattern of red and gold in the floor and a ceiling of circular tube lights that looked like a fleet of spaceships had invaded. At the gold-foiled ticket booths just inside, each guest was handed a bundle of rice nestled in a tiny square of white netting tied up with a satin bow, plus a commemorative booklet with pictures of all the actors and a story on Morgan. Derek had insisted on a story too, so he also got a full-page spread.

Velma gasped when they passed through the 6,500-square-foot Grand Foyer, gazing up at the 60-foot gold leaf ceiling that crowned the "Fountain of Youth" mural. In the center of the area stood an enormous eight-foot-tall tiered wedding cake for all the guests, who were also invited to the reception with the cast after the show. "I just hope we get to see Beauregard Buchanan getting someone in the sack," Enid giggled. "Great buns!" she added, causing the ladies to titter and blush.

Inside the cavernous auditorium, each of the aisle seats sported a nosegay of white roses and babies breath with a long, white ribbon flowing to the floor. The huge choral staircases on either side of the room also were strewn with nosegays and white ribbons. "This is going to be the most magnificent wedding ever!" Enid said, full of anticipation, as the ladies took their seats.

At 1:50, Bailey and Peter were sitting comfortably in the wings at the front of the stage with their closed-circuit TV, while Blaine and Mike ran themselves ragged, fussing over details. So far everything seemed to be working like a well-oiled machine—all the sets were functioning, the orchestra was playing.

"This is going to be so great!" Peter squealed, squeezing Bailey's hand. "Your crowning achievement as a soap writer."

A chubby guy dressed in jeans and a polo shirt straining at the seams came huffing and puffing from behind Bailey and Peter and stopped to catch his breath. "Is this the side where Set Number 1 is?" he asked.

"No, it's on the other side of the stage. But the extras aren't on until the second scene," she explained.

"Yeah, but I'm in the first scene," he said, wiping the sweat off his face," then excused himself and hauled his chunky butt across the stage.

The wheels in Bailey's brain came to a grinding halt. It couldn't be. Peter caught up about a second later. "That's Rock Hard?" he said in total disbelief. "He looks more like Poppin' Fresh!"

When Mike came over to the wings, Bailey glared at him, and he knew why. "You hired him over the phone, didn't you?" Bailey chided. "Couldn't you have taken a look at him before you gave him the job?" she shouted, getting to her feet. "It's been two years since he's been on the show, Mike! People can change a lot in two years, you know!"

"It never occurred to me—it just never occurred to me. We were in a bind, I had a thousand things going through my head, and I just told him to show up!"

Bailey looked at the rotund actor. "We can't put him on as Beau—look at him!"

"Well, who do you suggest we replace him with in the next three minutes?" Mike said, stating the obvious. "He didn't exactly have an understudy—he's the understudy!" Suddenly the overture began, signaling curtain time, and all three faces froze in panic. Mike ran off to take care of business; Bailey sat back down with a sinking heart; Peter took his seat, afraid to say a word; and at 2 o'clock on the dot, the shimmering gold curtain rose to thunderous applause.

෩

The cast had been told of Mitch's departure from the show when they arrived at Radio City that morning, so everyone had been expecting someone new. But the actresses in his one scene didn't get a look at him until they were actually on stage, which resulted in several unscripted facial expressions from Pashmina, who was the first to see him.

After Pashmina's exit, Aruba entered and knocked on Beau's door. When the new Beau opened the door wearing the Speedo with his white belly peering out over the elastic of his bikini, the actress tried to hide her shock. "W-e-e-e-ll," she stammered, knowing the words that would soon be coming out of her mouth didn't fit what she was seeing, but she had to continue nonetheless. "Don't...you look buffed and beautiful tonight. You must have sensed I was coming...or would be soon, perhaps," she forced herself to say.

The new Beau smiled with anticipation of what was coming next, but the only thing that rubbed against him was her hand when she pushed him away. "Are you going somewhere?" she asked upon seeing his suitcases in the bedroom.

"I'm leaving to sort things out, Aruba," he said, glancing at the cue cards for his next line. "I was all set to marry Pashmina, but," another glance at the cards, "now that you're pregnant with my baby—I have to figure out what's the right thing to do."

"Where are you going? Are you going back to your hometown?"

"No, I can't go back there—ever."

"Why not?"

Suddenly his eyes widened because the cue card that was on top was one he had already read from his scene with Pashmina. The stagehand recognized the look of terror and began shuffling the large white cards, searching for the right one, leaving the actor to his own devices. "Because...I was in trouble for something I did when I was younger."

Heather knew that line wasn't quite right and tried to steer him back to the correct story line. "You were arrested?" she said. "You never told me you'd been arrested."

Still no cards. "Well, I was!" he said like a 6-year-old trying to impress a buddy, "for something b-a-a-d!" When he turned dramatically away from the camera, he saw the stagehand holding up two different cue cards. His eyes frantically scoured them for his place, but neither was the correct card. "And now I can never go home again!" he said, gritting his teeth and shaking his head quickly at the stagehand, indicating those weren't the right cards. "If I do, they'll be waiting for me."

"Who?"

Finally the right cue card was found, but the flustered stagehand held it upside down, causing the actor to tilt his head, but it was no use—he couldn't read it.

He turned to the camera, and with a complete lack of emotion said, "Them," just before the music swelled dramatically and the camera came in for his close-up. Suddenly he remembered he was supposed to bite his hand in anguish, but in his nervous excitement, he bit too hard and yelped.

When the curtain came down, Heather stormed by the klutzy cue card guy and said, "Way to fuckin' go, butterfingers! My one scene today and you totally screw it up!" When she stormed by Poppin' Fresh, she grimaced. "And you—put some clothes on!" she snarled in disgust.

੨ঌ

The rehearsal dinner set rose to the stage, but by the time all the actors on the show were seated, there were only enough chairs for 11 of the 20 extras that had been hired for this scene. "I'm sorry!" Blaine snapped to the horde of fussing extras who had just lost out on a quick game of musical chairs, "we just don't have any more tables to set up!"

"But we told all our friends and relatives that we'd be on the show," they whined.

Blaine let out a sigh of desperation as he checked his watch, seeing valuable seconds ticking by. "I'll tell you what, you can be in the wedding scene as guests. There are already 20 extras in that scene, but there are plenty of pews in the back of the church to accommodate all of you." That cheered up the left-over extras. "But please, we need you back in the wings and out of the way now!" he said, hustling over to the set.

"But what do we do in the church scene?" one shouted after him.

"Nothing. Dab your eyes now and then," he said with a shrug, like any moron should be able to figure it out.

"Well, when do we exit?" the extra asked.

With only two minutes to go during this break, Blaine grew exasperated. "Just follow the principals when they exit!" he snapped, and rushed off to fix a centerpiece that had toppled over.

≈

The waiter approached and leaned in between the happy couple at the long table and delivered his line. Ace smiled sweetly at Binaca and said, "She'll have the beef Wellington, and—"

"—the older gentleman will just have warm milk and crackers," Binaca interjected, patting him condescendingly on the hand.

Derek and Morgan shot daggers at each other, with the unsuspecting waiter caught in between due to a momentary case of brain freeze. The only thing he could think to do was shuffle off backwards out of the camera shot, still smiling politely, to let these two carry on with whatever they were up to. This left Derek and Morgan locked in each other's glare. Morgan's eyes said, "First strike—I win, asshole!" Derek's eyes said, "You she-devil...the gloves are off."

After an awkward silence, Heather spoke up. "Oh, you two," she said, trying to save the scene, "you sound like an old married couple already," which prompted the best man to stand up, prepared to make his toast. But as he stood, Morgan interrupted with a trill of feminine laughter, drawing everyone's attention back to her.

"Ahh, that reminds me of the sweetest thing Ace did last weekend after a candlelight dinner. He said to me—" She stopped in mid sentence and patted Derek affectionately on the hand. "Oh, you tell it so much better than I—go ahead, honey," and she took a huge bite of her dinner roll to occupy her mouth, should he try to dump it back on her.

Derek was caught like a deer in the camera lights, his mind racing for words in front of a waiting audience, his armpits swimming in sweat. Bailey looked on from the wings in helpless horror. "My God—they've gone completely off-script!"

After what felt like an hour, Derek said, "Some things are meant to be private, my dear," then squeezed Morgan's hand so hard she gnashed her teeth in pain.

Peter shook his head. "This is like a bad episode of *Whose Line Is It Anyway?*"

Blaine signaled Zirconia to begin her speech to make up for lost time, and the matron of honor stood. "These two have known each other only a short time, and I'm guessing the groom doesn't know everything in Binaca's closets." The intrigued guests and the audience reacted accordingly.

"Ace, I'll bet you had no idea that your bride-to-be was once—

Derek slapped his hands on the table, surprising everyone. "A Las Vegas hooker!" he shouted as he shot to his feet. "Yes, yes—I know all about it!"

A collective gasp arose from the audience, and while Derek waited for the rumbling to dissipate before delivering his next line, Blaine took control and frantically signaled the orchestra leader to start "Blue Moon," cutting off Derek's impromptu dialogue.

Everyone applauded as the couple took to the dance floor, and the three cameras crisscrossed quickly to get into proper position for the close-up of Ace and Binaca cuddling and cooing.

"Binaca, my dear, your past doesn't matter a whit to me," Ace said sweetly. "I find it quite noble that even though you come from a wealthy family, you were so industrious about putting yourself through college."

Binaca smiled demurely.

"Yes, I know being a hooker isn't the most dignified profession, but you were young," he said. "This was something that happened a long time ago...a *very* long time ago," he said, causing Binaca's smile to go sour. "It just means we're going to have one helluva wedding night!" he said, then honked her right hooter, which was the one facing the audience. Six thousand voices stirred at various levels.

Derek's movement caused a chain reaction, and Morgan immediately latched onto his balls with her hidden left hand and squeezed them like a couple of lemons. The pressure caused his eyes to pop, and his voice mutated to Daffy Duck. "It just gives us something to look back on fondly as we grow old together," he quacked, as the music swelled for Ace's close-up kiss on her cheek.

But Morgan wasn't through yet. "Oh, Ace, are those tears of joy?" she said, grabbing his face with her other hand, squishing his cheeks hard as she jerked his face toward camera.

Bailey and Peter reared back at the hideous face filling the TV screen. The camera was in so close they could see the tears streaking Derek's makeup, his eyes now crossed in agony. "Not the most flattering close-up the man has ever had," Peter said, stating the obvious.

Derek grabbed Morgan's left hand and rescued his ball sac, then freed his face and grabbed her by the hair at the back of her head and laid a big wet one on her, right on the lips. The audience loved the kiss and went wild, applauding and cheering. Derek held her lips hostage until the curtain dropped, then she immediately pushed him away and wiped her mouth.

"Jesus Christ—did you stick a garlic clove between each tooth?" she shouted, then spit and wiped her mouth.

"I merely had lunch before the show at my favorite Italian restaurant," he replied innocently. "It was quite tasty...don't you agree?" he added in a taunting tone.

"I knew you were being too nice yesterday. I knew you would ruin my farewell show somehow—you shallow, egotistical bastard!"

"You started it today, with that 'warm milk' bit! And you deserve it too. You think you can just come in here with all your Hollywood glitz and glamour and take my show away from me?"

"Well, it was pretty easy to do—to take away a show from someone who's an impotent little fool."

The two faced off like a couple of WWF wrestlers. "Don't you dare!" he growled in warning, as they slowly circled each other.

"You better not screw up my big finale, I'm warning you!" she snarled back. "You stick to the script, or I swear to God I'll cut your dick off and hang you by your balls!" she threatened and stormed off.

As Morgan whizzed by, Peter turned to Bailey. "That woman has never had a cup of decaf in her life."

⋅⋅⋅

Morgan now had only three minutes to change into her undergarments for her next scene in the bridal dressing room, and in her haste she accidentally pulled off her panties with her black panty hose from the dinner scene. They were so knotted up in the nylon wad that she couldn't get them out, and finally the angry actress threw them aside with a snort. "Fuck this—I don't have time!" she said, grabbing her white panty hose and sticking her feet in.

After both legs were in, she stood up and shimmied the waistband over her hips. In the mirror, she noticed the unflattering pubic hairs matted in a way that reminded her of Chewbacca from *Star Wars*. And that horrid line where the panty begins that cut across the widest part of her thighs—ugh! She turned around to check her backside and snarled. "Good God—it looks like two hams stuffed in a dip sack," she moaned. "When did I get all those crinkles?" she said smacking her derriere, causing it to jiggle. "Thank God no one's ever going to see this side of me," she said as she dropped her floor-length slip, covering her butt with yards of white silk and lace.

⋅⋅⋅

The third scene went according to schedule, with only a few stray lines, and Morgan hurried back to the dressing room and grabbed some tissues, which she shoved down the front of her panty hose. Heather was a bit shocked and turned to give the woman as much privacy as was allowed in the open dressing room with a dozen women flitting in and out. "Good Lord, these nylons make you sweat without any cotton panties to absorb the moisture," Morgan said. "This is starting to chafe already."

"I have some FDS feminine spray, if you'd like a spritz," Heather said.

"Oh, no," Morgan said, "I don't use that stuff anymore."

"Why?"

"Because it's made mostly of cornstarch."

Heather didn't understand.

"Well, you know what happens when you combine cornstarch with moisture and heat?" she said, giving Heather a savvy look, but the younger actress had never been much of a whiz in the kitchen, so she just shrugged. "You end up making gravy," Morgan explained.

Heather grimaced at the disgusting image, then helped Morgan into her wedding gown. No sooner had she zipped up the bride when a production assistant poked her head into the room and shouted "Thirty seconds!" causing everyone to shift into high gear. Morgan and her two young flower girls rushed down the long hallway outside of the auditorium and climbed to the top of the choral staircase to prepare for her grand entrance.

The Mighty Wurlitzer had been providing soft music all through the commercial break, and when the appropriate moment came, Elton Johnson struck the chords at the beginning of the bridal march to announce the entrance of the bride.

The notes echoed through the gargantuan hall, providing the effect of a great cathedral. Those in the back of the auditorium saw Binaca first and began applauding, oohing and aahing, and soon all heads turned around to see what was happening. Everyone stood as the beautiful bride passed down the staircase, with her 10-foot train of beaded silk and lace held by two pretty little flower girls in their frilly dresses. Many audience members began weeping at the sight.

Soon Binaca took her place beside Ace at the altar. "Dearly beloved, we are gathered here today in the presence of God and all these witnesses to join together this man, Chauncey 'Ace' Atkinson, and this woman, Binaca Blaylock, in the bonds of holy matrimony. It is not a union to be entered into lightly..."

In the back of the church, one of the displaced extras nudged one of his fellow extras, looking somewhat distraught. "Who are the principals?" he whispered urgently.

Another extra sitting behind them leaned forward. "Yeah...aren't they all principal players?" he said, also confused by the brief direction given to them earlier.

The one who had been nudged replied, "I guess in this scene Ace and Binaca are the principals." They all wordlessly agreed that that made sense, then focused on the action once more.

"...Till death do you part," the preacher said.

Binaca slipped the ring on Ace's finger and

repeated the line, becoming agitated as the camera came closer.

"I now pronounce you man and—"

"*Stop!*" she shouted, to the surprise of the audience. "I can't go through with this! I can't do this to you, my love—I can't marry you!" she shouted, and rushed down the aisle, off the set, and toward the entrance of the bell tower, with Ace on her heels.

As the bridal couple dashed by the pews, one of the extras said, "Hey! There go the principals—come on!" and 12 extras in the back rows rushed after the bridal couple. The original 20 extras, who had been told to exit after all the wedding guests, decided they had misunderstood and also rushed out following their fellow extras.

Ace had his back to the staircase they had climbed up to the bell tower, and when Binaca turned to deliver her first line, her eyes popped, seeing two dozen extras trying to cram into the tiny bell tower with them. Derek noticed the strange look on her face and turned to see what it was. "What the blazes are you doing up here?" he snapped, momentarily forgetting this was a live show.

The group froze, since none of them had a line, until the pudgy woman in the center quickly became the spokesperson for the group. "Uh...we...thought the bride was going to throw the bouquet?" she said, hoping that would cover them.

Derek and Morgan scowled because that didn't make sense—the ceremony had never been finished—but to facilitate the situation, Derek angrily plucked the bouquet of orchids and roses from Morgan's hands and threw it like Joe DiMaggio at the gathered hoard, hitting the spokeswoman in the side of the head with the floral fastball. The extras took their cue beautifully and exited posthaste, with the woman cherishing her souvenir bouquet as she rubbed her watering eye.

In the audience, Bertha leaned over to Eugenie. "I know a lot of couples take out the word 'obey' from the traditional vows, but this is the first time I've ever heard of the groom tossing the bouquet." They shrugged, assuming they were totally out of the loop in today's MTV culture.

Morgan and Derek composed themselves quickly and proceeded. "I have something to confess to you, Ace."

"What?" Ace said, interrupting, causing Morgan to fear he might be about to go off on another improvised tangent. Warning daggers shot once again from her ice-blue eyes before she continued.

"I know you think I inherited my money from my father, but that's not true. You see...I was married before." The audience responded with shocked delight at the juicy tidbit. "And I got almost $10 million when he died."

"That's nothing to be ashamed of, my dear."

"But you see, he died of liver failure...which I induced by injecting him with concentrated vitamin A."

The revelation caused a tremendous rumbling from the audience.

"I don't believe you," Ace continued.

"It's true. I hated him! I wanted out of the marriage,

but he wouldn't let me have a divorce. He used to beat me every time I tried to leave," she said, becoming more distraught. "Finally I snapped and one night I killed him! I can't bear to have your reputation ruined and turn you into a social outcast in your hometown because you're married to a murderer!"

He took her by the hands. "But you had justification. And I'll never tell anyone. And in the future, if the authorities ever get suspicious, we'll get you the best attorney that dead bastard's money can buy."

Morgan reeled slightly at the "dead bastard" remark.

"No jury in their right mind would convict you after hearing all this."

"No! I can't," she said with building drama, "I murdered my husband, and I must be punished for it!" Binaca shouted as she climbed up onto the ledge. She turned to Ace and took in a deep breath—half for dramatic effect; half wondering whether Derek was about to use this last opportunity to screw her up by going off-script again. When he didn't, a wave of superiority washed over her, and she held her head high for her last line. "Goodbye, my darling Ace!" she said, then closed her eyes and leapt from the tower with a shriek, causing the audience to respond in kind.

"No, Binaca—*n-o-o-o!*" Ace cried, rushing to the edge, then turning away in horror. "I can't bear to look, to see the woman I love this way," he said, slumping to the floor, resting against the balustrade from which his love had just jumped.

But suddenly, from behind the grieving Ace, Binaca

bounced high above the bell tower, her wedding gown billowing out like a parachute on the way down, causing another gasp from the audience.

In the wings, Bailey was frozen in shock. Peter's hands went to his cheeks. "Sonja Henie's tutu!" he exclaimed.

"Oh, God," Derek went on, "I wish she could come back for just a few seconds," at which point Binaca obliged and bounced up again, arms and legs flailing, "so I could tell her how much I love her." This time Binaca was seen in mid air, facedown, like a parachutist waiting to pull the rip cord. The entire audience roared with laughter at the unexpected comedy routine.

Producers in the booth were going ballistic trying to pick a camera that wasn't showing the bouncing bride, but because Morgan was showing up directly behind Derek, who was the only one speaking in this scene, Morgan was in all of the shots. "Camera 1—focus on the sky behind the tower!" Mike shouted, but no sooner had the view switched to the blue sky than Morgan came bouncing into frame and through the airwaves into millions of homes across America.

"What the fucking hell is this?!" Bailey shouted as she took off running backstage behind the sets with Peter hot on her trail. She pulled back the side curtain just in time to see Morgan hit the trampoline sitting where the air mattress should have been. Poor Morgan looked like a perpetual-motion machine, each bounce feeding the next, tossing her high above the tower in full wedding regalia, to be viewed from every awkward, unflattering angle as Ace quietly continued delivering his lines to an audience now breathless with laughter.

"For me, she'll never really be gone," Ace said, as Binaca entered upside down with her butt crack showing, causing the crowd to burst out with a hysterical laugh.

"I'll always have that last, lingering image of her today in her beautiful bridal gown," he said, right before the bride appeared for the last time, upside down, legs straddled to showcase Chewbacca in all her glory, with the beautiful wedding dress falling down and completely covering her face.

Bailey wanted the floors to open up and swallow her alive. "Well, there goes my career," she said as she heard the curtain being lowered to a torrent of laughter and applause.

A couple of stagehands managed to wrangle Morgan to a stop, and she crawled awkwardly over the side of the trampoline. Once on the hardwood floor, her legs were shaking so much she had to be steadied by one of the men. Bailey came up and grabbed her arm. "I'll take it from here," she said, and the two union men left in a hurry, repressing their laughter.

Morgan wadded up two big handfuls of satin and lace. "I swear to God, every time I put one of these damn things on, my life turns to shit!" she screamed, then let go of the dress in a violent motion, like she was throwing something disgusting away.

"Come on," Bailey said, trying to guide Morgan toward the front of the set, "you have to take a curtain call."

Morgan planted her feet like a couple of 300-year-old sequoias. "There is no way in hell I am going to show my face to that audience!" she shrieked.

"Why not?" Derek laughed, "They've already seen your best features." He laughed even harder.

Morgan was so angry at Derek for setting her up she couldn't speak, which was a first for her, and he managed to escape, laughing hysterically, to take his curtain call.

"Is this how you want it to end?" Bailey asked. "If you don't go out there and take your curtain calls, everyone will be laughing at you...just like Derek. But if you go out there and act like it was planned, and hold your head high, they'll laugh with you."

Somewhere deep inside Morgan knew Bailey was right, but she was so filled with humiliation and hatred for Derek, she wasn't thinking clearly.

"Be bold, be brave," Bailey said, holding her chin up in example.

Morgan took a deep breath and closed her eyes. "Well...I can only hope that on camera the panty part of the stockings was dark enough that I can get away with saying I was wearing a dark thong panty underneath."

"Or you could be sassy and say this was your way of saying 'fuck you' to the network for dumping you so callously," Bailey suggested.

Morgan decided she would think about it later, because she knew Bailey was right about what she had to do right at this moment. The actress removed her arm from Bailey's grasp and walked to the center of the stage on her own, the continuous applause from the other side of the curtain still echoing.

Morgan went on for five full minutes thanking her devoted fans for coming from all parts of the country, endearing herself to them all, ensuring her popularity for future endeavors, playing the theatrical politician to the hilt. The audience applauded feverishly, chanting for one curtain call after another.

After the final curtain, Morgan grabbed Bailey by the sleeve and dragged her to the dressing room. "Come on, sister, let's screw the reception and blow this joint. We'll go to my apartment to celebrate getting dumped from this turkey! We'll take it like a couple o' broads."

Chapter Seventeen

"So what are you going to do?" Morgan asked as she poured Bailey a glass of champagne. "Stay in New York...go to L.A.?"

"Actually, I wouldn't mind a change of scenery," Bailey said as she sipped from her glass, standing by the vast windows of Morgan's elegant penthouse apartment. "And I could do without these nasty New York winters, that's for sure. I don't know, I haven't really had much time to think about it. What about you?" she said.

"Luckily I've had dozens of offers since they announced my departure from the show—everything from a Broadway play to a movie in England. But there's an hour-long family drama on one of the other networks that appeals to me too, so I've just been waiting for a sign," she said, walking over to Bailey. "I'm just thankful I've got several options."

Bailey shrugged. "I figure that if an opportunity

doesn't present itself pretty soon, I'll just make my own opportunity," the writer said.

Morgan admired the tall woman sipping champagne. "I believe you will, Bailey." She threw back the rest of her drink and ran a fingertip around the edge of the glass absentmindedly until the crystal sang. Then she placed the empty glass on a Louis XV table and said, "Speaking of opportunities...I have an opportunity to do something right now that I may never get the chance to do again, and I really don't want to pass it up."

"What's that?" Bailey said, expecting to hear about another career option.

"This—" Morgan replied, wrapping her arms around Bailey and kissing her full on the lips. During the long, lingering kiss, Bailey wondered if it were the alcohol and stress getting to the actress, but when she felt Morgan slip her the tongue and run her hand over Bailey's ass, she knew this woman meant business. Overwhelmed, Bailey pulled back.

Morgan read the stunned look. "Yes, dear Bailey, I like my lovers the way I like my jackets—double breasted. Always have," she said frivolously. Then she got serious.

"You have to remember, I grew up in the days of the studio system, when guys like Jack Warner and Louis B. Mayer ran every aspect of their stars' lives. And the studio publicity department handled the press—we very seldom dealt directly with the media, so the publicists concocted those very public lives for us. And quite often those lives weren't anywhere near the truth," she said solemnly.

"I felt like such a hypocrite, but it just wasn't safe back then. Being gay would absolutely kill someone's career in those days. So they set up sham marriages for people like me. Only I couldn't put up with the bastards they picked for me for more than a couple of years at a time—it was just awful living with someone I didn't love and didn't even know, actually.

"Then in the '60s, the studio system fell by the wayside, but it still wasn't safe. So after that, I kept up the ruse and arranged a few marriages myself. I mean, can you imagine what would have happened to me if I'd made fools out of millions of men who had drooled over me in their fantasies over the years? And millions of women who had envisioned me as the ideal woman? There wouldn't have been a corner of the earth far enough away for me to hide in if I'd done that."

Bailey understood perfectly. "God, that must have been an awful way to live. But, how did you—" She was about to ask how Morgan managed to have lesbian lovers for decades without anyone finding out, but she stopped, feeling like she was prying.

"How did I have a sex life?" Morgan said, sensing the aborted question. "It wasn't easy. But that's what those big ol' Beverly Hills mansions with the high brick walls are for...so no one can see what really goes on inside. But after my last divorce two years ago, I said enough. I made up my mind that the next relationship I got in, I'd come clean and tell the whole world the truth."

"Are you sure that's what you want to do?"

Morgan held her head high. "Sweetheart, I've lived

my entire life pretending to be other people...I think it's time I start being me," she said with total assurance. "I've just been waiting for a woman strong enough to handle going through that with me."

Bailey felt something in the air but wasn't quite sure what. "Do you mean me?"

Morgan laughed. "There's no one else in the room." She sidled up to Bailey again. "I've really fallen for you over the last year...are you surprised?"

"Stunned is more like it."

"Why? You're a strong woman, you're intelligent, funny, sensitive, talented, and successful. I admire those qualities. And I like the way you stood up to me about keeping the wedding scene in. I need a big, strong shoulder to lean on now and then." She stroked one of Bailey's shoulders. "And yours seem to be just about right," she said, then slipped her arms around Bailey's waist and hugged her, which led to another, more passionate kiss.

"Plus, I figure I'm old enough now that not too many men will be that disappointed to find I'm not available for their fantasies," the actress said.

"You look great, Morgan," Bailey said, admiring her face and figure. "You're still a beautiful woman."

The actress' smile became animated. "Yes...thanks to Dr. Rosenthal, I still have a great set on me!" She shimmied her tits in an enticing manner, making Bailey blush. "God only knows at what latitude these babies would be hanging if it weren't for good ol' Doc Rosenthal."

Bailey giggled, but she couldn't help tingling all over

at being invited to look at Morgan's fabulous breasts instead of having to sneak a peek, as she had done so many times at the office.

"I gather by that smile on your face you like my figure?"

Bailey's face went red-hot. "As a matter of fact, I have noticed it on occasion over the last year," she confessed, looking away, feeling shy.

Morgan became self-conscious and turned away, also. "Yes, I've had a few nips and tucks over the years," she said, then became defensive. "Well, you have to if you want to keep working in this business—this disgusting, well-paying business. And thank God it is well-paying, otherwise I'd have starved between jobs this last decade.

"Speaking of being out of work," Morgan continued, "I've been thinking about you." Bailey was touched by this. "I figured that since you've been fired too, there's a chance you might become homeless soon and need a roof over your head. I've got more money than I could spend in three lifetimes...I can certainly take care of you," she said suggestively.

Bailey was completely flummoxed by the events unfolding—too many emotions colliding all at once. "Oh, I couldn't let you support me. I'd feel like a gigolo. And you can imagine what all the tabloids would say. But thank you," she said with appreciation.

"You can't let me take care of you...or you can't live with me as my lover?"

A grin spread across Bailey's face at the thought of being Morgan Gable's lover. "I just meant the first."

"Good," Morgan said, kissing the woman on her cheek. "In that case, I think I know how to fix this situation."

Morgan sat on the red-and-gold damask couch, where she picked up the phone and dialed a long-distance number. "Raymond Abernathy, please...Morgan Gable..."

Bailey recognized the name of the president of one of the other networks and was impressed that Morgan was being put through to him.

"Hello, Raymond, how are you...just fine, listen, I've decided to accept your offer of the prime-time drama series...yes, I think it's a wonderful opportunity too, but there is one thing I'm concerned about...it's the writing...it just doesn't 'zing,' if you know what I mean...well, I'd like to bring my own writer on board...Bailey Connors, she's the head writer on *All the Bold Days*..."

Morgan looked up at Bailey, wanting to know if this met with her approval. Bailey shrugged as if to say "Why not?" Morgan smiled at Bailey, pleased.

"Yes, she does have great talent...anyway, she did so well with my character over the last year, and we've worked so closely together, I just feel she knows me better than some Hollywood hack who happened to write a good spec script for no actress in particular...well, regardless, I feel strongly about the situation, Raymond...yes, I'm afraid this is a deal-breaker..."

A long pause ensued as he considered the situation, but Morgan gave Bailey a wink, indicating she felt she had the battle won.

"Wonderful," Morgan finally said with a Cheshire

cat smile, "I'll have my agent call you tomorrow and we'll start working out the details...you too, Raymond, dear...goodbye."

Morgan stood up and threw up her hands. "Hollywood, here we come!" she said with delight.

The two drank a toast to the new adventure they were about to embark on together and sealed the toast with a kiss. Bailey looked deeply into Morgan's blue eyes. "You have no idea how many times I dreamed about kissing you," Bailey confessed.

"Just kissing?" Morgan said playfully.

"Well, I suppose I have thought about touching this incredible body of yours now and again too."

"Well, you know what they say...there's no time like the present," she said, and started walking Bailey toward the bedroom. "You know, one of the reasons I've kept my figure so well is because I've never had children. Do you have any idea what having babies does to a woman's body?" she asked, now standing in front of her four-poster bed.

Bailey grimaced as thoughts of a recent conversation at an Italian restaurant came back to haunt her. "As a matter of fact...I do."

"Then you should appreciate these," Morgan said as she placed Bailey's hands on her large, firm breasts and squeezed until she felt Bailey taking over. Then she wrapped up the big woman in a kiss, and reached over and pushed the bedroom door closed.

About the Author

Sharon Stone is the author of the best-selling novel *Love Letters in the Sand*. She began her writing career as a screenwriter in Los Angeles. As a journalism graduate of the University of Missouri-Columbia, she later became a bureau chief/columnist for the *Tampa Tribune*. Currently she writes, produces, and directs for her company, Hi-Brow Productions, and is a member of POWER UP. She also taught screenwriting at the University of South Florida. Visit her Web site at www.hi-browproductions.com.